WAHIDA CLARK PRESENTS

ALONG CAME A
SAVAGE

A NOVEL BY

JOE AWSUM

WITH WAHIDA CLARK

This is a work of fiction. Names, characters, places, and incidents either are the product of the author's imagination or are used fictitiously, and any resemblance to actual persons, living or dead, business establishments, events, or locales are entirely coincidental.

Wahida Clark Presents Publishing
60 Evergreen Place
Suite 904A
East Orange, New Jersey 07018
1(866)-910-6920
www.wclarkpublishing.com

Library of Congress Cataloging-In-Publication Data:
Joe Awsum
Along Came A Savage
ISBN 13-digit 9781944992682 (paper)
ISBN 13-digit 9781944992897 (ebook)
LCCN: 2017914952

1. North Carolina- 3. Drug Trafficking- 4. African American-Fiction- 5. Urban Fiction- 6. Prison Life

Cover design and layout by Sebastien Stewart | seb@15-23.com
Interior design by NuanceArt@aCreativeNuance.com
Edited by Linda Wilson
Proofreader Rosalind Hamilton

Printed in USA

WAHIDA CLARK PRESENTS

ALONG CAME A SAVAGE

A NOVEL BY

JOE AWSUM

WITH WAHIDA CLARK

Chapter 1

Good Girl Gone Bad

Club Roxy was a hot new club on Chicago's South Side. Its elegance brought out all the ballers across the city, and tonight was no different. Bottles of Rosé Moët poured like bottled water after a track meet, as the males showed off their net worth by seeing who was going to buy the most bottles, especially since it was ladies' night.

Ladies' night always brought out all the bad bitches. They were coming out of the woodwork in every size and complexion. Most of them were dressed like the strippers who were going up and down the twenty stripper poles throughout the club.

"Bitch, I don't know how I let you drag me out tonight," a pretty, light-skinned female said to her brown-skinned friend.

"There you go, Tay Tay, you always tripping. Bitch, you can't tell me this spot ain't turnt up."

"I ain't gon' lie, Mesha, you always know where the turn up at."

"Bitch, that's what I do. Ain't shit changed since I moved away. I know it's been awhile since you been able to come out and play, so I wanted to make sure we did it right."

"You the one who disappeared."

"Hell, nah, bitch, you got with Mr. Ivy League Drug Lord and didn't even realize I was gone."

"First off, I was caught up in school, and Wayne is far from a drug lord."

"Bitch, please, he like the king of Chicago."

"Whatever!"

"School sure ain't paid for them diamonds on your wrist," Mesha said as she looked at the lights flickering off of Tay Tay's diamond ring and bracelet like a disco ball.

"Wayne ain't been in no streets; he been investing in real estate and business."

"Bitch, who you talking to? I been around you since we were little girls, and you know damn well, I *know* better." Tay Tay had almost forgotten that she was talking to her best friend and that Mesha knew her and Wayne's life like a book. She hadn't seen her in a year and a half, and Wayne had trained her to tell anyone that asked about his occupation that he was into real estate and owned businesses, even though he was the city's biggest cocaine and heroin supplier.

Tay Tay was about to reply as she attempted to gather her thoughts but was interrupted.

"Excuse me, ma, can a brother buy a fine lady like you a bottle?" a dark-skinned man with dreads said.

"I'll pass, I'm married," Tay Tay said before sipping

from her glass of Hennessey.

"Damn, shorty, a nigga just trying to get to know you."

"Damn, nigga, you can't hear or something? Shit, do it look like we need a damn bottle? We good, nigga!" Mesha said before pouring the remainder of one of the three bottles of Moët they had on the table onto the floor, splashing on the dark-skinned man's shoes.

"First off, I ain't even talking to you. She a grown woman. She got a mouth of her own."

"Like I said, I'm married, now please move. You're blocking our view," Tay Tay said, knowing Mesha had no chill.

"Yeah, a'ight. I'll see you around."

"Doubt it. Now *poof*! be gone, nigga!" Mesha said before taking a swig from one of the two bottles of Moët she had left. The dark-skinned man just nodded his head slightly before walking away.

"Girl, you still crazy."

"Bitch, you know that sure ain't gon' change. But, anyways, when you get married? And even better, why the fuck wasn't *I* invited?"

"It ain't even like that. It was a spur-of-the-moment thing. I went on a trip to Vegas with Wayne, and the next thing you know, I was married," Tay Tay said, knowing she had taken off her ring to avoid this conversation tonight.

"Whatever, bitch. Anyways, let's toast to the bride then," Mesha said, holding up one of the remaining bottles of Moët for a toast. Tay Tay grabbed the other bottle and toasted with her best friend before gulping from it. Tay Tay was happy to be back around her girl. Lord knows she had so much going on in her life that she wanted to talk to Mesha about, but now wasn't the time. She hadn't had fun in a long time, and she wasn't about to waste a moment of it talking about her problems. Instead, she guzzled some more from her bottle.

***

The club didn't close until 5:00 a.m., but Tay Tay and Mesha left around two in the morning. They were drunk and starving as Tay Tay parked her white-on-white BMW 745 down the street from the hot dog stand so they could get some Jew Town polishes.

"Bitch, I'm about to buy everything on the menu," Tay said, passing Mesha the Backwoods full of loud they had been smoking on the ride there.

"Hell, yeah, you ain't never lied," Mesha said, giving her girl a high five.

Tay Tay and Mesha got out of the car trying to pull their tight miniskirts down over their curves. Both of them were thick like most of the video vixens you saw on TV. They only took a few steps when they heard a voice from behind them that made them stop and turn around.

"All I wanted was to get to know you. Then this bitch fronting me off in the club like I'm a sucka nigga or something," the dark-skinned man with the dreads from the club said.

"What the fuck! You some type of stalker or something?" Mesha asked.

"I'm sick of you bougie-ass bitches thinking you all that.

I could buy both you hoes," the man said, throwing a handful of dollars at them like they were some strippers. Tay Tay was about to say something before Mesha's temper came out, but they were interrupted by a voice coming from behind them.

"Nigga, you got a problem with my wife? Hold my food, boo," a light brown-skinned man said, passing Tay Tay his food before kissing her on the cheek. Tay Tay had never met the man before, but something made her play along with him.

"It ain't even like that, fam."

"Well, it's like that now, nigga!" the man said before pulling his gun from his waistband and pressing the barrel of it against the man's forehead.

"Please! It's all a misunderstanding."

"You damn right, it's a misunderstanding. Now tell my wife and her friend, you sorry."

"I swear, I'm sorry."

"Y'all accept his apology?"

"Hell, nah, fuck him!" Mesha yelled out.

"Yeah, yeah, we forgive him," Tay Tay said, not wanting to get the man killed. She found herself turned on by this man defending her honor.

"Get the fuck out of here!" the brown-skinned man said, putting his gun back up. The dark-skinned man didn't say another word. He just turned and ran away.

"Well, I hate to get married and divorced on the same day, but I got an after-party to attend," he said. Tay Tay found herself hypnotized by his green eyes and muscular arms that were covered in tattoos.

"Bitch, say something," Mesha said, nudging her.

"Yeah, my name is Tay Tay and this my girl, Mesha. Thanks for helping us," Tay Tay said, snapping back to reality.

"It ain't nothing, sweetie. My name's Sa'vere. Look, since we're getting divorced, we might as well go out with a bang. Let me get y'all's food, and then I'll escort y'all to the celebrity after-party downtown. I heard Kanye and Drake supposed to fall through. So, what y'all say?"

"Bitch, he said Drake. Now you *know* he your favorite," Mesha said, excited.

Tay Tay hesitated for a second before speaking. "Fuck it, let's do it," she said. She had told Wayne she was staying in Chicago with her aunt for the weekend, especially since he wasn't fond of her hanging out with Mesha, or anyone else, for that matter. She knew it might be awhile before she saw Mesha again, so she planned on making the most it.

***

The line at the downtown hotel was almost wrapped around the building as Sa'vere, Tay Tay, and Mesha walked up.

"We ain't never gonna get in here. You know what, we appreciate you helping us tonight, but maybe this was a bad idea. Here, let me get you the money for the food," Tay Tay said, digging in her white Louis Vuitton purse.

"Chill, shorty, we good, trust me," Sa'vere said, pulling his phone out of his pocket and dialing a number. It rang for a few moments before someone answered on the other end.

"I'm outside," was all Sa'vere said before hanging up the phone.

"What's going on? I'm ready to get it poppin'," Mesha said.

"Well, y'all follow me then." Sa'vere walked them around to the dark alley behind the club. Tay Tay was ready to leave, but the back door of the building opened. Sa'vere shook the big security guard's hand before giving him a semihug like they'd known each other from way back.

"They with me."

"Well, you ladies better come on in," the security guard said, holding the door open for the women. The ladies followed closely behind Sa'vere as they walked through the kitchen while the kitchen workers continued working.

The third-floor penthouse suite was full of celebrities and the people who were lucky enough to get in.

"We 'bout to go to the ladies' room," Mesha said, grabbing Tay Tay by the arm.

"Okay, I'm about to get us some drinks," Sa'vere said, rubbing his 360 waves like he was brushing them as he looked Tay Tay in the eyes like no one else was in the room.

"Come on, girl, damn," Mesha said, pulling Tay Tay away. The line at the bathroom took almost twenty minutes to get inside. When Mesha's turn came up, she and Tay Tay went in together. Mesha turned the water on and went into her purse and pulled out a sandwich bag full of colorful Ecstasy pills. She quickly untied the bag, took out a pill, and popped it into her mouth before cuffing some water out of the running faucet in her hand and swallowing her pill.

"Damn, Mesha. What the fuck you on?"

"Bitch, quit playing. Take a Wonder Man."

"Girl, I don't know about that shit."

"Bitch, you said that the first time I gave you a blunt. Trust me . . . damn."

"Fuck it!" Tay Tay said, taking the pill from Mesha and swallowing it down. Mesha was two years older than Tay Tay and was always influencing her into doing stuff.

"Damn, bitch, you gotta live a little. This place is full of stars, and I'm about to catch me one."

"Whatever!" Tay Tay said, knowing her night was about to be next level fucking with Mesha.

The next couple of hours was full of liquor. Tay Tay didn't know if she was feeling the liquor or not, considering her pill had kicked in. She was having a ball, and before she knew it, she found herself just hanging with Sa'vere like she was his girl at the party as he was mingling with everyone.

"I need some air," Tay Tay said, feeling her body heating up from the Ecstasy.

"I got a suite here if you need to get away from all this craziness. These celebrities take partying to the next level."

"You know where Mesha's at?"

"After Kanye showed up, I ain't seen her since."

"Let me call her. I gotta make sure she straight. We came together, we leave together," Tay Tay said, pulling her phone out of her purse and pushing SEND on Mesha's number. The phone rang once before Mesha answered with loud music playing in the background that wasn't the same as Tay Tay's.

"Bitch, where the fuck you at?"

"Girl, I seen Yeezy. I'm on his heels."

"I'm about to go get some air. Call my phone if you need me."

"All right, girl, I gotta go. You interrupting my mission," Mesha said before hanging up.

"Well, I guess she's good. Let's go get some air."

The suite Sa'vere was in was pure luxury. She wouldn't have guessed that a street nigga like Sa'vere would be in a place like this. She wanted to ask him what he did for a living just out of curiosity, but she was a pretty good judge of character and could tell that he was a drug dealer.

"This place is nice."

"Thanks, this is some last-minute shit, but it'll do," Sa'vere said, laughing.

"It sure will do. This place gotta be $1,000 a night."

"It's $1,200, but I've seen better. This uppity shit ain't me. My peeps wanted me to come party, and that's what I did. Shit, you can give me a scale and a Motel 6 any day."

"I feel that shit."

"You smoke?"

"Hell, yeah!" Tay Tay said, wanting to smoke some weed badly, hoping it would calm down her Ecstasy high.

"Good, let's smoke this uppity muthafucka out."

"Well, let's do it then," Tay Tay said, loving a real nigga that made his own rules.

For the next hour, Sa'vere rolled blunts of loud, and they

smoked like they weren't in a high-class room. Tay Tay had been telling herself she was going to smoke a little more, and then leave. She knew she had no business alone with a man this fine and gutta like she liked. His conversation had her wrapped up; plus, it had been months since Wayne had been traveling the country on business and hadn't been around to talk about life or simply touch her. Tay Tay didn't know if it was the pill's side effect, but she found herself leaking in her panties just looking at Sa'vere.

"Damn, what time is it? I think I need to be finding Mesha," Tay Tay said as they finished the second blunt.

"It's 4:30."

"Damn, it's late."

"I understand. Well, it has been nice being married to you for a day."

"It's been nice being married to you as well," Tay Tay said, giving Sa'vere a hug as they approached the door. The hug was meant to be short, but Tay Tay found herself holding onto his muscular structure. *Bitch, get out the door*, she thought, but her body was saying, "take me now." Sa'vere pulled away just enough to look deep into Tay Tay's eyes like he was reading her soul. Tay Tay hesitated at first, but before she knew it, her lips were pressed against his. Their passion was like an explosion, their tongues meeting, the fuse that ignited it. Sa'vere picked her up off her feet, and her thick thighs wrapped around him instantly as they continued to kiss. She didn't know where Sa'vere was taking her, but she was ready to go.

Within minutes, she found herself on the granite countertop in the kitchen.

"Oh shit, what am I doing?" Tay Tay whispered out loud as Sa'vere began sucking on her neck aggressively before pulling her perfect titties out of her tight shirt. He took those titties and pushed them together before sucking hard on both erect nipples, back and forth, until Tay Tay was moaning slightly. The way he moved his tongue, she couldn't do anything but wonder how it would feel on her dripping-wet pussy. She didn't have to wait long to find out as Sa'vere pulled her white lace panties to the side and dove face-first into her ocean of pleasure.

"Oh my God!" Tay Tay yelled out as Sa'vere's tongue flicked across her swollen clit.

"God ain't gonna save you. Bitch, feed me that pussy!" Sa'vere said before diving back into her sweetness. Sa'vere's words made Tay Tay want to come everywhere. Before she knew it, she was holding both cabinet handles with her feet flat on the countertop as she fucked his face.

Sa'vere accepted the challenge as Tay Tay continued grinding her pussy in the air and all across his tongue. His arms cuffed her thighs and lifted her off the counter, all the while still eating her pussy as she held onto the cabinet handles.

"Oh shit, you gonna make me come everywhere!" Tay Tay screamed out as her body began convulsing, come leaking out of her pussy and into his mouth. Sa'vere didn't give her a chance to recover. He just picked her up and threw her across his shoulder like a caveman. Tay Tay had never been manhandled like this before and every second of it had her wanting to be fucked even more. Sa'vere threw her on the huge bed, and he watched her like a wild animal eyeing at his prey. Tay Tay bit her bottom lip as he took his shirt off before pulling his rock-hard dick out of his pants. He rolled a condom on, and before Tay Tay could blink, he had snatched her to the end of the bed and plunged his big dick deep inside her tight, wet pussy. The pleasure outweighed the pain, and Tay Tay couldn't do anything but grab the sheets for the ride.

"Damn, you feel like you in my stomach."

"I'm about to get all in this phat-ass pussy," Sa'vere said, grabbing her by both her ankles, spreading her thick thighs all the way apart as he stirred in that pussy like some macaroni. His stroke was slow at first, but his aggression took over after about a minute, and Tay Tay found herself getting fucked like never before.

"Oh shit, nigga, you killing this pussy!" Tay Tay screamed out as she began coming again . . . and again as he continued to beat that pussy like it stole something. Sa'vere pulled his dick out and flipped her over before digging inside her dripping-wet pussy from the back. He showed her no mercy as he pounded her from the back. Tay Tay had to bite the bedsheets to stop from screaming his name to the heavens above.

Tay Tay was happy when Sa'vere reached his climax, and she couldn't do anything but lay across the bed. She looked back at him, and he was standing there like a savage. That was the last thing she remembered before passing out.

***

Tay Tay woke up around 7:00 a.m. The effects of the Ecstasy wouldn't allow her to stay asleep, but the ringing of her phone was what woke her up. She was half-dressed as she looked around for Sa'vere, but she didn't see him. Then she heard the shower running and saw the bathroom door was cracked. She hopped out of the bed and went to the bathroom door and peeped inside. She could see Sa'vere's silhouette through the steamy glass shower doors. She quickly ran and got her phone out of her purse and went into the kitchen. She calmed herself down before dialing the number back that had already called four times.

"Good morning."

"Morning, Wayne."

"I called you a bunch of times. Is there something wrong with your phone?"

"I was asleep."

"I told you no matter what time I call, you gotta answer this phone, Taylor. This ain't no game. Anything could be happening, and your fucking excuse is you were fucking sleeping. This is unacceptable!"

"I know, Wayne. I was up late taking care of my aunt."

"Well, get yourself together and get home. I need you to do something for me."

"Okay."

"I hope your aunt gets better," he said before hanging up in her face. Tay Tay hated Wayne's voice at that moment. She knew he didn't care about her aunt and was just saying that to be funny. She put her phone on the counter and walked back toward the room. By the time she got to the bedroom, she was butt naked and headed straight for the bathroom. It was steamy from the hot water as she entered the room. She walked like a woman with purpose as she opened the shower door.

"Let me help you with that," she said, watching the water drip off his dick. He became hard instantly looking at her sexy body. Tay Tay didn't give him time to react. She knew what she wanted, and she was going to get it. She grabbed his swollen dick and stroked it before squatting down eye-to-eye with the dick. Sa'vere looked down at her as she took him in her mouth slowly, then slurped on it like she would a Popsicle in the summertime. Tay Tay looked up into his eyes as she continued to jerk his rock-hard dick off on her thick, wet lips.

"Bitch, quit playing and suck this dick," Sa'vere said, grabbing the back of her head and pushing his dick back in her mouth. She moaned slightly, loving his aggressive nature as his dick pounded against the back of her throat.

"Damn, girl, I'll fuck you all in your mouth," Sa'vere said, grabbing her head with both hands. Tay Tay wanted that dick all down her throat, and Sa'vere was giving her what she desired, and more. Tay Tay could taste come leaking into her mouth, so she pulled his dick out and continued stroking it as she put his balls gently in her mouth.

"Shit, bitch!" Sa'vere said, loving the freak in Tay Tay. Tay Tay took his balls out of her mouth, then began licking her tongue up from the bottom of his shaft until she reached the head, making come squirt out in her face and mouth like a volcano had erupted.

"Shit!" Sa'vere moaned, putting his hand against the wall for balance as she sucked the head of his dick making sure she got every last drop.

"Now, we officially divorced," Tay Tay said, standing up and walking out of the shower.

Sa'vere couldn't do nothing but shake his head looking at all that ass walking out of his shower. He was going to let her walk away but couldn't. Tay Tay had just got out of the bathroom when she heard the sound of Sa'vere walking fast behind her. She turned around just as he got to her. Suddenly, she was up in his arms with her legs wrapped around his waist. He took both of them straight to the bed. His dick slid right into her wet, throbbing pussy. He grinded all in that pussy until her nails were lodged in his back.

"Oh, Sa'vere, you keep hitting my spot, daddy!"

Sa'vere could feel her pussy pulsating around his dick, so he began speeding up until you could hear Tay Tay's pussy leaking. Her thighs trembled hard around his body, and her nails in his flesh made her look like she was holding on for dear life.

"Right there, right there. Oh shit, I ain't never felt like this. I'm about to come all over that big-ass dick." No sooner than the words left her lips, she had come running all over his dick. Sa'vere really began beating that pussy hard and fast, making Tay Tay scream out and begin shaking again.

"Oh shit, nigga, I'm coming again!" Sa'vere could feel her wetness increase and had no choice but to pull his dick out and come all over Tay Tay's pussy. *"Now* we're divorced, bitch."

"Whatever, nigga," Tay Tay said, lying there as her body continued to tremble in pleasure. Sa'vere found himself shaking his head again, knowing he had broken his number one and number two rule, but he liked it.

***

"Well, you be safe. If you ever change your mind about divorcing me, here's my number." Tay Tay looked at the piece of paper Sa'vere was holding as he leaned in her window.

"I guess. Bye," she replied, taking the number like she didn't want it before letting the window up on him. He could see her smiling through her tinted window as she backed up. Sa'vere just stood there with a devilish grin on his face, watching her pull off. As soon as her BMW disappeared in traffic, a voice from behind got Sa'vere's attention.

"Damn, nigga, what the fuck is you doing? We got shit to do."

"I'm coming, Trell. Shit. Quit sweating me, nigga," Sa'vere said, talking to the dark-skinned man with the dreads that he had pulled the gun on last night for Tay Tay and Mesha.

"Nigga, you over here all glossy-eyed and shit, watching the bitch leave. Nigga, don't fuck this money up."

"Nigga, get your ugly ass in the car. I know what the fuck I'm doing. When have I ever missed my target?" Sa'vere asked, pausing, waiting on Trell to answer.

"Exactly. Now get your ass in the damn car."

"Nigga, fuck you!" Trell said, getting in the car with his best friend. He knew Sa'vere was a ladies' man and made both of them a good living doing it.

"That bitch just like the rest, nigga; this money in the bank," Sa'vere said with his million-dollar smile. Being a professional side nigga wasn't his career of choice. It was a career that chose him. He knew there was a lot of money on the line with Tay Tay. He had already violated two of his own personal rules of his hustle which was never have sex but one time on the first night, and never ever have unprotected sex. Both of those built too many emotions and, in this game, there was no room for feelings or fuckups, especially at this level. Last time he had fucked up, it got him stuck in this career. Sa'vere knew Tay Tay was on his mind, and he couldn't deny it. He was going to have to shake the shit off because shit was about to get real. Lighting a cigarette, he blew the smoke out the window as he and Trell made their way through traffic.

Chapter 2

Touched by a Savage

It had been two weeks since Tay Tay had been in the city. Wayne had kept her extra busy, especially since he had expanded his network to Texas. Tay Tay had gone to school for accounting at Northern Illinois, and that's where she met Wayne and why she was so key to his operation. When they first met, he was far from a drug dealer. He was handsome and smart, and going to school for business. Some would've thought he was a nerd, but Tay Tay felt the same about herself since she was the only one of her friends who got straight As through high school and went to college. They had plans of opening up stores and being in business together when they graduated. That ended up coming true, but it didn't come in the way they imagined. Upon their junior year in college, Wayne's older brother put him onto the cocaine hustle. Wayne was the opposite of his brother and knew nothing about selling drugs. Luckily, Tay Tay had grown up around cocaine, so she helped him. Wayne was the black man that fit in with the white crowds, and that was the key to their come up. By the time they graduated, Wayne's charisma and Tay Tay's dope hustle had them with over a million dollars and three businesses.

Now, they were bringing in about two million a week and owned more businesses than Tay Tay could keep up with. The more money they made, the more businesses they opened to hide it, and Tay Tay was the best at that. At times, she felt like that was the only reason Wayne was with her. They used to be so in love, like they were living a fairy tale, but the last few years, Wayne had let the money and the power change him. Tay Tay held on for the money and the hope that the needy thug she fell in love with came back to her, but she knew Wayne was nothing but a white dude trapped in a black man's body; his pungent, uppity attitude proved that every day. She only saw glimmers of the man that used to treat her like a queen, and that only came after he was making up for his abusive ways. She had wanted to tell Mesha, but she didn't want to darken their weekend. She had been tempted to call Sa'vere after the way he made that pussy feel, but a little piece of her felt guilty considering that was the first time she ever cheated on Wayne, *and* the first time she experienced an orgasm. The thought of the abuse he put on that pussy made her instantly wet as she sat behind her desk in her home office. She found her hand sliding up her thighs, ready to put her fingers to work inside her wet pussy, but a voice made her stop instantly.

"Taylor, did you book my flight like I told you?"

"Of course, Wayne."

"Well, cancel it. Tell them I need the private jet gassed up now."

"I thought your meeting wasn't for two days. I was thinking me and you could go out for dinner tonight and have some fun like we used to."

"You must not have heard me. Call and tell them to get the jet gassed up. I don't have no time for fun when I got the biggest deal of my career at hand. I'll be gone for a week since we moved the meeting up, so that means get on your phone and get to work and quit asking me questions. I don't know what your fucking problem is lately. You need to get your head back in the game, because there's a million bitches ready to be in your position," Wayne said as he finished tying his tie before walking out of the room. Tay Tay hated Wayne at times, and this was one of them. She took out her phone and pulled up a number that said "Auntie," then sent a text message that said, **Can I see you?** Tay Tay sat impatiently looking at the phone's screen and at the room door, hoping that Wayne didn't pop back in. Suddenly, she heard the chime of her messenger notification going off. She pulled the message up and all it said was when and where.

Give me an hour, and I'll tell you, she texted back.

A few seconds later, a text came back that said, **I'll be waiting.** Tay Tay almost came on herself right there in her chair knowing she was about to see Sa'vere again. She had told herself she wasn't going to use his number, but she saved it under Auntie just in case she needed it.

"Fuck you, Wayne! You the one gonna fuck around and get replaced," she said to herself, sitting back in her $3,000 leather chair like the boss that she was.

***

O'Hare Airport was packed on a Friday night, but Tay Tay didn't worry about any of that as her black-on-black Maybach pulled up to the private airport hangar. She had booked herself a private jet for tonight after booking Wayne's, which flew out of a private airport in Waukegan where he moved a lot of his product through. She was rich and only twenty-eight, and she was about to start acting like it. She knew Wayne was going to be somewhere with his rich friends, some white bitch on his arm, titties in his face, while he and his friends did business. She planned on doing him the same way from now on, she thought to herself as she watched a black Cadillac limo pull up, Sa'vere getting out of the back.

"Well, damn, this how you do it," Sa'vere said in his black and red suit that Tay Tay had sent for him, along with the limo.

"Well, you did show me a good time and had me and my girl's back the other night, so I thought I'd return the favor. Besides, we need to look over our divorce paperwork," she said, looking at him seductively. Seeing her thug in a suit made her pussy want to jump out of her panties.

"I totally agree," Sa'vere said as he looked at Tay Tay who had on a skintight Louis Vuitton dress that matched his suit. Her straight, shoulder-length red hair hung past her shoulders.

"Your flight is ready, ma'am," the pilot said to Tay Tay.

"Thanks, here we come," she replied to the pilot as he walked off before speaking to Sa'vere. "You don't want to know where we're going?"

"It's looking like I'd follow you to hell," Sa'vere said, watching her like a top sirloin on his dinner plate.

"You gon' get enough of looking at me like that, 'cause I'm going to give you what you're looking for."

"I hope so, 'cause I'd hate to have to take it," Sa'vere replied before giving Tay Tay a devilish grin.

"You ever been to Vegas?"

"Nope."

"Well, I guess I made a good decision then. You know what they say . . . What happens in Vegas stays in Vegas." Tay Tay smiled back before turning around and walking toward the G6 private luxury jet.

Sa'vere couldn't do anything but follow her and that phat ass that Tay Tay was throwing like a champ as she walked. Sa'vere told himself to calm down because this situation was turning out to be bigger than he imagined. The luxury G6 was even more luxurious than he'd seen on TV. The seats were made of plush Italian leather, and there was woodgrain everywhere. It was more like being in a luxury suite than a jet.

"Can I get you a drink, ma'am?" the white, blond stewardess asked, standing in the aisle between Tay Tay and Sa'vere's seat.

"Yes, I want a glass of Moët with a strawberry in it."

"And for you, sir?"

"Hennessey."

"One shot or two?"

"The whole bottle."

"Right away," the stewardess said before walking off to get the drinks before takeoff.

The next thirty minutes, the two drank their drinks and small talked about how they had a good time the last time they were together.

"Can I get you another drink, ma'am?"

"Yes, thank you," Tay Tay said before looking at the white stewardess's phat ass in her short black dress as she turned to walk away. Sa'vere caught her looking in the process of looking himself. They both just laughed like they could read each other's nasty minds. Tay Tay hadn't felt so free in years, and with Sa'vere, she planned on enjoying every moment, she thought to herself while watching him drink his Hennessey out of the bottle.

***

Sa'vere had been to a lot of places in his line of work but never to Vegas. Once the plane landed at the private hangar, they exited the plane to an awaiting red Lamborghini.

"You know how to drive one of these?"

"Boo, I can drive anything," Sa'vere said, taking the keys from the car escort's hand. Both doors were up on the Lamborghini as Tay Tay and Sa'vere got inside. The automatic doors came down, and, soon, Sa'vere peeled off out of the parking lot.

"Where are we going?"

"To the top of the world, I hope."

"Well, make sure you buckle up because this ride ain't

for no amateurs."

"I been buckled in, nigga," Tay Tay replied making them both laugh as Sa'vere whipped into the heavy night traffic.

They had enjoyed the night air of the Strip as they pulled up with the top down at the Bellagio Hotel. "Let me go check on our suite. I'll be right back," Tay Tay said, looking at him seductively before getting out of the car, ready to get the party started. She hadn't been there in almost two years since she and Wayne got married. They had spent their honeymoon at the Bellagio. It wasn't much of a honeymoon, though, since Wayne didn't even get the chance to touch her since he had to leave in the middle of the night on business. Tay Tay had spent the next day alone, pampering herself. Wayne had told her he was going to make it up to her but never did. It was okay, Tay Tay thought to herself, because she was about to have a honeymoon of her own tonight.

"How may I help you, ma'am?"

"Yes, do you have a reservation for Washington?"

The white desk clerk typed in the computer, looking for the reservation.

"Yes, what's your first name?"

"Taylor."

"This is strange. It says you and your husband, Wayne Washington, checked in an hour ago. Do you need a key to your room?"

"No, that's okay. I'll just find my husband. I'm sure he has an extra key already," Tay Tay said with a smile trying to hide her anger and hurt. She knew Wayne's ass was up to no good, talking about "the meeting was moved up."

"If you need anything, let us know. Enjoy your stay."

"I sure will," Tay Tay said, walking away. "Oh, I'm *definitely* about to enjoy my stay," she said, thinking out loud. She was ready to go find Wayne's dog ass and see what bitch he was with, but then remembered she was doing bad too. And to think, she almost felt guilty calling Sa'vere.

"What's wrong?" Sa'vere asked as Tay Tay got in the passenger seat with a straight face.

"Nothing, daddy," she said, pulling herself together real quick.

"Well, what's the plan, sweetie? Everything straight with the room?"

"Yeah, we good. I just changed my mind on rooms. I figure we here, we might as well do it big. We gonna go down the street to the Palms."

"It's whatever, baby, so long as I'm with you."

"You gon' stop playing with me, nigga."

"I don't play with nothing but pussy," Sa'vere said, pulling off as Tay Tay called the Palms Hotel on her phone and put it on speakerphone.

They answered after a couple of rings. "Thanks for calling the Palms Hotel; how can we help you?"

"Yes, I want your most expensive room."

"Our most expensive is the Hugh Hefner Sky Villa."

"And how much is that?"

"$40,000 a night."

"Well, can I get three nights for $100,000?"

"Yes, yes, of course. How will you be paying for that?"

"Black Card. I'll be there in five minutes. My name is Taylor Washington."

"No problem, ma'am. We're awaiting your arrival."

"Thanks, see you soon," Tay Tay said before hanging up. "You ready for this life?" Tay Tay asked, ready to live life again. She had two million put up that nobody knew about, a million in her savings, and two million in a joint account with Wayne. Wayne had paid for everything over the years, and she just stacked her money. She was ready to enjoy her wealth and Sa'vere at the same time. Wayne could be a thing of the past, so it was time to start investing in her future, she thought to herself, smiling, as she stared into the city lights.

"Hell, yeah," Sa'vere replied, feeling like a boss as he switched gears in the Lamborghini like a NASCAR race car driver.

Sa'vere had remembered seeing the Hugh Hefner Sky Villa on TV but never imagined that he would be standing in it.

"Greetings, I am your personal butler, Ted. I will be here to make your stay as relaxing as possible. If there's anything I can get you two, just ask."

"We're looking to party this weekend. I'm sure you can make that happen, huh?" Sa'vere said, giving Ted a hundred-dollar bill.

"Not a problem, sir. I can assure you when I say I can get you anything, I mean *anything*. This is Sin City, after all."

"That's what's up, Ted, I like you already," Sa'vere

said, holding his hand up, making Ted give him some dap before he walked off.

Tay Tay loved a hustler with swag, and Sa'vere was turning out to be all of the above. She found herself in his arms, her lips pressed against his. The short passionate kiss ended by Tay Tay hugging Sa'vere tight, like she never wanted to let go. Tay Tay was hurting inside over Wayne, and Sa'vere was her only medicine.

Sa'vere hugged her back tightly like he could feel something was wrong. He knew he was getting too wrapped up in Tay Tay too quickly, but for some reason, it felt so right.

"What you say, we go down to the casino and fuck up some commas?"

"I'd say, let's do it, daddy," Tay Tay said seductively, already feeling like her life was a gamble at this point.

***

Sa'vere and Tay Tay spent the next few hours in the casino. Sa'vere had been breaking even on the crap table all night. Tay Tay wasn't too fond of the table games, but found a quick addiction to the slots. She had started playing the quarter slots and had worked her way up to the five-dollar slots.

"I swear this my last time, baby," Tay Tay said to Sa'vere as she gripped the handle, ready to hit the slot one more time.

"You said that thirty minutes ago," he said, laughing.

"Whatever, nigga, come on over here and help me."

Sa'vere walked up behind her, wrapping his arms around her before resting his hand on top of hers.

"This roll for us, nigga, a'ight?"

"A'ight," Sa'vere said, nodding his head in agreement and digging Tay Tay's style at the same time.

"Well, let's get it, then," Tay Tay said, pulling the handle with Sa'vere. Sa'vere was focused on Tay Tay's phat ass up against him and didn't realize they had hit the jackpot until bells and sirens started going off.

"Oh shit, you gotta be fucking kidding me!" Sa'vere said, looking at the $50,000 jackpot sign light up.

"I knew I made the right decision," Tay Tay said before turning around and kissing Sa'vere passionately. She knew she'd made the right decision on playing the slots one last time, *and* on being with Sa'vere.

Winning only increased their passion toward each other. All the way to the room with their winnings, they could barely keep their hands off each other. They found themselves kissing as they stood next to the minipool that extended like a glass balcony overlooking the city.

"I hope you can swim, nigga," Tay Tay said before starting to undress herself.

"Bitch, I'll drown on purpose in between them thighs."

Tay Tay took her clothes off until she had stripped down to her red lace thong and matching bra set. She looked at Sa'vere seductively as she walked toward the table and grabbed the $50,000 in cash off of it. She held a stack of cash in each hand as she walked toward the water. Hundred-dollar bills fell to the ground with each step like she was leaving a path for Sa'vere to follow.

Sa'vere didn't hesitate to strip down to his black boxers and grab the bottle of Hennessey Paradise off the floor. He followed Tay Tay's phat ass and the trail of hundred-dollar bills to the pool. The view from the extended glass balcony was worth the hefty price tag. The view of the city was breathtaking, but so was Tay Tay, Sa'vere thought as he approached her in the water. He took a big swig from the bottle while looking in her eyes.

"Hold this, and gimme that," Tay Tay said, passing him a stack of the money she was holding before taking the bottle from him. She put it to her lips and hit it just like he had. He smiled as she gave it back to him. He took one more shot before setting the bottle on the side of the pool. "Is you scared of heights?" she asked.

"I ain't scared of nothing!" Sa'vere said as Tay Tay backed up to the edge, leaving a trail of hundreds for him to follow.

"You think this is a lot of money? I can change your life in more ways than one."

"Oh, yeah?" Sa'vere said as he walked up close to her as her back touched the glass wall of the balcony pool, leaving her nowhere else to go.

"Yeah," Tay Tay replied before they began kissing aggressively. As they stopped, Tay Tay nibbled on his bottom lip like she was biting it.

"You make me feel some type of way, nigga, I swear."

"Bitch, quit playing with me," Sa'vere said, leaning in again and kissing her. Within seconds, his dick was sliding inside her as the kiss became more intense by the second.

"Make this money rain on us while you fuck me,

daddy," Tay Tay said before throwing the stack of money she was holding up in the air. Sa'vere didn't hesitate to follow her lead before digging deep inside her. She grabbed him tightly as he pounded that pussy with her back against the glass wall overlooking the city. The hundred-dollar bills rained from the sky like Magic City on a Monday night. Some of the bills blew away, out of the window and over the city, but the rest fell in the water and on Sa'vere and Tay Tay like a money shower. Sa'vere showed her no mercy and continued to bang her back against the wall until she was coming uncontrollably, back to back to back.

"Damn, you making me love you, nigga," Tay Tay said, throwing that pussy back, trying to meet the challenge.

"This my pussy?"

"Yes, daddy, it's all yours, I swear."

"It better be," Sa'vere said, about to pull his dick out as he felt ready to bust.

Tay Tay's body began losing control, and she couldn't stop from coming again, with the thought of Sa'vere busting his load all in her pussy. She felt his dick ready to bust as he was pulling out, but before he could, she threw that pussy back hard on the dick until she could feel the warmth of his come inside her. She lay her head on his chest as he continued to hold her against the wall. He kissed the top of her head, holding her tight as he looked out over the city, knowing he had now broken *every* code he lived by. But for some reason, he was still wishing that she was his.

***

The next morning, Tay Tay was up early headed to Walgreens to get a morning-after pill. She was happy they sold them over the counter because she wasn't trying to go home pregnant, even though Sa'vere felt so good inside her. She ended up buying a few extra because she planned on having a lot more sex with him.

She was about to get in the Lamborghini when she thought she spotted a familiar face.

"Mesha!" Tay Tay yelled, seeing what looked like her best friend dressed like a prostitute, trying to call for a cab. Mesha heard Tay Tay and turned around.

"Tay Tay, bitch, what you doing here?" Mesha said as she approached her girl, giving her a hug.

"Nothing, girl, just having a little fun."

"Bitch, who you here with?" she asked, knowing the devious look on Tay Tay's face.

"Sa'vere."

"Bitch, you lying! What about Wayne?"

"We gon' need to have a long talk. But enough about me, what is you doing here? I been calling you since the party in the city."

"I'm with one of my ballers. You know how we do. I had lost my phone and just got a new one."

"Well, fuck it. We in Vegas together, might as well have a ball. You and your friend gotta come party with us."

"Damn, bitch, you sound like the Tay Tay I know. He must be giving you some good dick."

"Girl, you have no idea. That's why I'm down here now, getting me a morning-after pill."

"Bitch, you lying."

"Shit got crazy last night. Come on, let's go get some food and talk."

"You in this?" Mesha asked, looking at the Lamborghini.

"Yeah, it's a rental."

"Yeah, bitch, let's do this," Mesha said as her door came up so she could get in.

They rode around the city for a minute, enjoying the feeling of success. They had always said when they were younger that they were going to be rich and come to Vegas, and here they were, riding around in a Lamborghini.

"Why is Wayne here with another bitch in the same hotel we had our honeymoon in?"

"Bitch, you lying. Fuck that shit! Where they staying? We going there now and tear that muthafucka up!" Mesha said angrily.

"Girl, he ain't even worth it. He been on some bullshit for a long time. I smell the perfume on his suits and seen plenty of lipstick on his collar and underwear."

"Why you put up with that shit?"

"I don't know, girl. I guess I love him. When he hit me, I thought about leaving but I couldn't walk away from all that we built. "

"Fuck that bitch, I'm gonna stab his ass next time I see him."

"Fuck that nigga. Right now, I just want to do me. I feel like I'm me again."

"*That's* what's up, girl. I'm happy to see you back. I was starting to worry about you for a minute. You disappeared and left me behind."

"It wasn't even like that; trust me, girl. You my best friend. I love you so much, you don't even know. Trust and believe, I'm back. He wants to play games—I can play too."

"Hell, yeah, bitch!" Mesha said, giving her girl a high five.

"Party on me tonight, girl. I'm sorry I left you."

"Fuck that shit, girl. We good, trust me. I ain't about to turn down no party. Where we partying at?"

"Don't trip, I'm 'bout to show you. It's still Pimp Squad Forever."

"It will *always* be Pimp Squad Forever!" Mesha answered back. Pimp Squad was the name of their clique growing up, which consisted of Tay Tay, Mesha, and Stacey. They had prided themselves on getting ballers for money. The clique fell apart when Tay Tay went away to college.

"Did you go to Stacey's funeral?" Tay Tay asked.

"Yeah. They had to have a closed casket for her. Shit was really messed up. You know you should've been there."

"Girl, I was in Europe. I didn't find out until I came back. I felt bad as hell. I sent her mama twenty thousand to help out. I still don't know what happened."

"She was messing with the dude that owned the club I took you to. Next thing I know, she was found in her car full of bullets."

"Damn . . . What the police saying?"

"They said it looked like a gang hit, but they ain't got no leads or witnesses."

"That's fucked up. When they gonna find out something?" Tay Tay asked, pulling up in front of her hotel.

"Damn, bitch, this where you staying?" Mesha said, changing the subject.

"You ain't seen shit yet. I'm happy you here, Mesha. I missed you."

"I missed you too, bitch. Now enough with this mushy shit. Let's see what this fancy muthafucka look like," Mesha said as the valet approached her door.

***

"I ordered us breakfast!" Sa'vere yelled out from upstairs, hearing the butler downstairs opening the door.

"I hope there's enough for me!" Mesha yelled back as Sa'vere emerged at the top stairs with some shorts on and no shirt.

"Look who I found, baby. She coming to party with us."

"Hell, yeah, that's what's up."

"Come on, girl," Tay Tay said, taking Mesha to the glass elevator to go up to the second floor. The table looked like a minibuffet when they got upstairs.

"Well, damn, there's enough food for everyone, and then some. Looks like y'all been having a good time," Mesha said, looking at the hundred-dollar bills on the floor and floating in the pool.

"Girl, we 'bout to turn up tonight!"

"Sa'vere, what's up with the party?" Tay Tay asked.

"I'm about to get on that right now. You beautiful ladies sit down and enjoy all this food."

"We sure will, I'm starving," Mesha said, sitting down.

Sa'vere made his way to the bedroom and closed the door behind him, leaving the ladies to themselves. He picked up his cell phone and dialed a number.

"Big Meat, I need a favor."

"Nigga, where you been? I ain't seen you since the damn party. We got some more security jobs coming up, and I'm going to need you."

"I gotcha, nigga, trust me."

"You always say that. Now, what you need?"

"Who you know in Vegas want to party at the Sky Villa tonight?"

"Shit, me, nigga. Fuck you doing in Vegas at the Sky Villa?"

"It's a long story. You know I'm gonna fill you in."

"You stay on some bullshit."

"Nigga, you gon' help me out or not?"

"Now you *know* I am. I need to make some phone calls, and I'll get back to you."

"I need a DJ too."

"Is that all?"

"Yeah."

"Good," Sa'vere's friend said, digging before hanging up. Big Meat was the security guard at the party that Sa'vere took Tay Tay and Mesha to. He is also one of his closest friends and gave him jobs to work, which got him access to celebrity parties where he found a lot of his female targets. Sa'vere just sat on the bed and grabbed the bottle of Hennessey Paradise he had left from last night and gulped it down, knowing it was about to be a long day and a longer night.

***

Breakfast hit the spot, and they were all full sitting at the table that still had a lot of food on it.

"Well, I needs to be getting back to my friend. He probably worried about me."

"Hold on, I'll give you a ride."

"I'm good. I'll definitely be back, though."

"I'll call you so we can go shopping. You know we gotta be on fleek tonight."

"Hell, yeah, bitch!" Mesha said, pushing the down button on the elevator.

"Nice meeting you again, Sa'vere. You better treat my girl right, or it's going to be me and you, nigga."

"Trust me, she in good hands," Sa'vere said, pulling Tay Tay close to him and hugging her.

"I guess," Mesha said, getting on the elevator.

"So, that's your best friend?" Sa'vere asked.

"Yep, since we were eight."

"That's what's up," he said, hugging her before kissing her on her forehead.

***

Mesha walked out of the hotel fast like she was aggravated. A cab was already outside. "Where to, ma'am?" the cabdriver asked.

"The Bellagio," Mesha said, sitting back in her seat with a devilish grin on her face.

Chapter 3

Trust Issues

Putting together a party at short notice was not Sa'vere's specialty, but you wouldn't have guessed it by the crowd that showed up to the Sky Villa. Big Meat had come through for him big time. He had Lil Wayne, Floyd Mayweather, Future to make an appearance, and even got DJ Drama to DJ. The butler got them all the party favors they needed from weed to pills, and females.

"Where's your date, girl?" Tay Tay asked, looking like a million dollars in her red Louis Vuitton catsuit.

"He had to leave on business."

"That's fucked up."

"Fuck it, girl, I'm about to turn up in this bitch. Thanks for the outfit. I'm going to slay in this bitch," Mesha said in her red skintight Divenchy dress.

"I told you not to worry about nothing, I'm back, girl."

"Well, I'm about to go and try to let Lil Tunechi get some of this coochie. He don't do nothing but make babies. Might as well get me one of them little rich muthafuckas."

"There you go. You see Sa'vere?"

"I saw him going outside looking for you."

"Damn, girl, I'll be back."

"A'ight, girl, I'll be here somewhere," Mesha said smiling as Tay Tay walked off.

Mesha waited until she saw her girl leave the villa before walking off to find who she was looking for. It only took her about five minutes to locate him. Mesha walked right up to him and tapped him on his shoulder.

"We need to talk right now," Mesha said, looking at Sa'vere like she was pissed.

"Excuse me, I'll be right back," Sa'vere said to the people he was mingling with before escorting Mesha through the crowd. Sa'vere walked her toward a bedroom, then stepped inside. Mesha shut the door behind them as he turned on the light. As soon as the light came on, Mesha grabbed him and started kissing him aggressively. He grabbed her phat ass from underneath her dress as she tried to get his hard dick out of his pants.

"Hold up!" Sa'vere said, pulling his lips away.

"Fuck that, daddy, don't you miss me? I miss that dick all in my mouth," Mesha said as she kissed on him and continued trying to undo his pants.

"You know I miss you, Mesha. You 'bout to get us caught up, though. Where's Tay Tay?"

"She's outside, looking for you, nigga. Now quit playing with my dick and give me what I want," Mesha said, pulling his dick out before getting on her knees and putting it down her throat.

Sa'vere stood there as Mesha deep throated that dick

like she was trying to knock her tonsils out. It didn't take her long before Sa'vere bust his load deep in her throat.

"You better remember whose dick this is. When you done breaking this bitch, your ass coming home where you belong. You remember what happened to Stacey, nigga."

"Now you know I'm on straight business. Look around you."

"Fuck that. This bitch all at the store buying the morning-after pill and shit. Y'all making love on money and shit."

"Mesha, you 'bout to fuck this shit up being all paranoid and shit. How the hell you get seen anyhow?"

"Wayne's bitch ass wanted some damn cigarettes, talking about he don't smoke at home around Tay Tay. When I saw her in the store, my cab had already pulled off. Next thing I know, she calling my name."

"Damn, that's crazy. What happened to Wayne?"

"I sent him back on his original trip to Dallas. He played his part. I knew that bitch would go back to that hotel. Wayne's pillow-talking ass told me how he left her there on their honeymoon. She's too predictable. She fell right into your arms like I said she would. Don't play no games, baby. Get that money so we can live like this just like we planned."

"I got this, Mesha."

"I hope so," she said, wiping her lips as she walked out, leaving Sa'vere standing there.

"I need a fucking drink now," Sa'vere said, thinking out loud, knowing this situation was becoming more and more complicated by the second. He knew he was in love with

Mesha, but Tay Tay was something different. He regretted letting Mesha get him involved in this side-nigga hustle. But he couldn't even fault her when he was her side nigga once upon a time. Sa'vere zipped his pants and buckled his belt before turning the light out and returning to the party.

The party was one for the ages, and it didn't turn down until almost six in the morning. Tay Tay and Sa'vere had popped a pill before they disappeared into a bedroom. Sa'vere wanted her badly, and he didn't hesitate to bend her over a chair in the room. He peeled her out of her catsuit and dug his dick right around the side of her red thong. He was on that pussy like it was his first time getting some, making her scream out in ecstasy. They were so caught up in their lovemaking that they didn't hear the door crack open.

Mesha had played asleep and couldn't resist going in to peep on Tay Tay and Sa'vere. Watching the way Sa'vere was pounding her friend made her pussy begin throbbing. Before she knew it, her fingers were in her panties playing in her soaking-wet pussy. She pressed her fingers inside her pussy hearing the sound of Tay Tay screaming in pleasure.

"Fuck that bitch with my dick, daddy," Mesha whispered to herself as she finger-fucked her pussy like it was Sa'vere.

"Oh shit, I'm coming!" Tay Tay screamed out. Mesha couldn't hold herself back either, and her body began trembling as she came all over her fingers. Gently, she eased the door closed and tried to gather herself for a few seconds after tasting the come off her fingers. "Enjoy it while you can, bitch. This about to be my life!" Mesha said to herself before walking off. She would have loved to stay and play, but she had an early flight to Dallas.

***

The weekend had been memorable for both Tay Tay and Sa'vere. The flight back to Chicago was spent talking about where they were from and what their lives were all about. They were captivated by each other, and the chemistry was undeniable. Sa'vere had told her he grew up in Chicago as a kid but moved to Texas and was just now coming back.

"So, you still haven't told me what you do for a living."

"A little bit of this and a little bit of that," he said looking out the window of the Maybach.

"Sounds like fun. Maybe I can contribute to it."

"Maybe," he said, looking over at her and smiling.

"Well, there's something I want to tell you, and I hope it doesn't run you off because I really do want you in my life."

"What's up, Tay?"

"I'm married."

"Damn, I ain't know that. I sure ain't trying to break up no happy home. Niggas be crazy these days."

"Trust me, he is far from crazy over me. I swear you ain't got nothing to worry about."

"I ain't never been in no situation like this before, but I also never met nobody that makes me feel the way you do, either. Any man slipping on you don't deserve a lady like you." Tay Tay almost melted out of her panties right at that moment.

"I love you, Sa'vere!"

"I love you too, Tay Tay!" he said before they began kissing passionately. Tay Tay didn't know where the words "I love you" had come from, but she was happy he returned them. She hadn't felt anything like this in a long time, and she wasn't about to lose the feeling for nothing.

"This is where I'm staying."

"This raggedy hotel?"

"Told you I'm just getting back. This hotel is how I eat every day. Every hustler has to start somewhere. A phone, a scale, and a Motel 6 is all I need."

"Well, this can be your trap house but not the one you lay your head at, boo. I ain't trying to knock your hustle or nothing, I just don't want nothing to happen to you. I need you, Sa'vere."

"I ain't trippin', sweetie, I can feel what you saying. I'm trying to be around for you too, but what I'm supposed to do?"

"Let me be your trap queen."

"Well, every king needs a queen."

"Good, nigga, 'cause I'd hate to have to cut you."

"Me too. I don't want no trouble, just some of that phat-ass pussy," Sa'vere said with a devilish grin on his face.

"You so damn nasty. Well, don't trip. We gonna have plenty of time for that. I'm going to call you in a little while. I got some stuff to put together. Ain't no way my king going to be living like this."

"It's whatever, baby. I'm a soldier. I'm cut for this shit."

"I know, boo, but trust me, I got us," Tay Tay said, kissing him on his lips before he got out of the car.

Tay Tay was going to go straight home, but she

detoured and made her way to the West Side of Chicago. It wasn't often that people came through driving a Maybach, and you could tell by the look of the kids' faces as she pulled up in front of her childhood home.

Tay Tay walked up to the porch and right through the door even though she hadn't been home in two years. The smell of chicken frying filled the air.

"Alisha, you early; the baby sleep," a voice yelled from the kitchen. Tay Tay didn't say anything as she walked into the kitchen.

"Girl, you ain't hear me say the baby is asleep."

"I heard you, Mama."

"Tay Tay," said a brown-skinned lady with a cigarette between her lips and a greasy fork in her hand.

"Hey, Mama."

"Get your ass over here and give me a hug."

Tay Tay was around the table and into her mother's arms like a little girl.

"I'm sorry, Mama."

"It's okay, baby. You better not ever disappear like that again, 'cause if you do, I'm going to have to fuck you up."

"Okay, Mama, I won't. I promise."

"Good, now sit your ass down so you can get a home cooked meal. I'm trying to get this party together."

"A'ight, a party for who?"

"A party for me," said a voice from behind her.

"Oh my God, Snoop, you home!"

"You damn right!" her brown-skinned twin said. Tay Tay ran to his swollen arms and dove right into them.

"When you get out?"

"This morning."

"Damn, I missed you, boy."

"I missed you too, sis."

"Look at you, all swole and shit. Last time I seen you, you had a fade. Now your shit's almost longer than mine."

"This is what five years in max looks like." He glanced at her hair. "Yeah, my hair might be a little longer than yours."

"Whatever, nigga," Tay Tay said, hitting him playfully.

"Well, this a picture-perfect moment, but since we ain't got no camera, this E&J gon' have to do," Ms. Brown said, hitting her cigarette and grabbing the bottle off the table.

"Mama, we gonna have to upgrade you to Hennessey."

"Boy, shut up. I made you off E&J. It's in your bloodline."

"Mama, you play too much," Snoop replied, laughing with his sister and mother. They crowded around the table and picked up their shot glasses their mama had poured.

"To family!" Ms. Brown said, holding up her glass. They followed her lead before drinking their shot.

"Well, ain't this one big happy family," a brown-skinned girl said standing at the kitchen door.

"Hey, Alisha," Tay Tay said seeing her little sister.

"Hey, Alisha, hell! Don't come around here now, acting like you ain't run out on me and Mama. I know all about your drug empire."

"Alisha, that's enough."

"Naw, Mama. She needs to hear this shit 'cause where was Miss Goody Two-Shoes when the lights were cut off, and we ain't have no food? You got a lot of nerve showing up here. Where's my baby so I can get out of here. I thought today was a celebration."

"He's asleep. Don't go waking him up with no mess. I know you twenty-one, but this my damn house, and you gon' respect it or get checked."

"Whatever, Mama. You want to babysit, fine then. Call me when she leaves. Bruh, I'll come kick it with you later. I ain't got no time to be fake."

Tay Tay just stood there looking at her sister in shock. She was more shocked by how Alicia had grown up on her, than how she was talking to her. Tay Tay knew she deserved what she was hearing because it was true. Besides, she was six years older than Alisha, so she needed to be the bigger person.

"Yeah, I love you too," Tay Tay said, making Alisha really mad before she walked off.

"I see you still know how to push her buttons."

"I ain't even worried about her."

"She just blowing off steam. Shit did get bad here for a second. One thing you can never do is turn your back on your family, because at the end of the day, we all you got."

"I know, and I'm sorry, I swear."

"It's okay, sis. All that matters is we here now. Alisha big-head ass will come back around."

The bedroom door opening got their attention. "And who is this little fella?"

"Jabari, come here. There's somebody I want you to meet," Ms. Brown said to her three-year-old grandson as she went and picked him up.

"Say hi to your auntie, Tay Tay," Ms. Brown said,

passing Tay Tay the little boy.

"Hey, little man. You know you too cute. Auntie is going to spoil you to death," Tay Tay said, kissing him on his cheek. Tay Tay was nervous about coming home. She had dreaded and wondered what the day would be like when she finally did. Now that it was over, she felt like a weight was lifted off her shoulders. Wayne had kept her busy and away from her family intentionally, and she knew it, but she had nobody to blame but herself. She vowed to make it up to her family as she kissed her nephew again.

***

Tay Tay decided to stay the night, and they reminisced on old times. After they finished the fifth of E&J, they went to the store to get another. By midnight, Tay Tay and her brother found themselves sitting on the front porch like they were kids again. Only this time, they had a half-empty fifth of E&J between them as they watched the neighbors and street niggas enjoying the night air.

"Man, I know I should've come to see you or even write you. I just—"

"It don't matter, sis, fuck that shit. I love you, and I know your heart. I'm your twin, remember? I'm proud of you, though, sis. Had a damn Maybach out here and shit. I been hearing about things on the inside. You'd be surprised how fast gossip travels when you locked up."

"So, what's your plans, bruh?"

"Get me some bitches, then go get the money the street owes me. These niggas been eating long enough. I'm thinking about fucking with Ted that own that new strip club everyone's talking about."

"Fuck that nigga. I heard he got something to do with Stacey getting killed. You been gone for a while. These niggas move a little different now," she said, knowing her brother had already done five years for a home invasion.

"I'm sorry to hear about Stacey. But you think I'm worried about these niggas? I'll fuck one of these niggas up for this bread and over you, and that's on everything," Snoop said, pulling out an all-black .40-caliber handgun from his grey prison jogging pants.

"I know, Snoop, just be cool. I want you home. Give me a day, I'll get you right. When we get up, we going shopping. We need to focus on you getting some pussy and not killing somebody." Tay Tay knew her brother was dead serious about killing somebody over her, so she thought it best not to talk about her Wayne situation. Besides, she was just happy her brother was home and didn't want to get him pissed off, especially while he was on that E&J. She grabbed the bottle and turned it up, wishing she could just drink her problems away.

***

The back of the Laundromat was quiet as the heavyset, clean-shaven, dark-skinned man walked in the room. His diamond-encrusted chain and pendant that said Big Dawg flickered off his all-black shirt that matched his jeans and shoes. Wayne, his brother, J Mo, and Mesha were sitting in the chairs at the desk.

"Hey, Big Dawg, I want to introduce you to my boyfriend, Wayne, and his brother, J Mo. These the ones I been telling you about," Mesha said, getting up and giving Big Dawg a hug.

"It's nice to meet you, gentlemen. My sis, Mesha, done spoke highly of you two," Big Dawg said, shaking both men's hands.

"Pleasure is all ours," J Mo said, speaking for himself and his brother.

"Well, let's get down to business then. Mesha tells me you're looking for a new supplier?"

"Yeah, we're looking to expand our network. What we're being offered now for the quantity we're trying to get ain't in our best interest at this time," Wayne said.

"So, what we talking? Ten to twenty bricks?"

"How about 100 to 200?"

"Shit, that's a lot of weight."

"If it's too big of an order, we're sorry for wasting your time. No disrespect, but we were told you were the man to see," J Mo said.

"Well, that person told you right. I'm the King of Dallas. Don't shit move unless I say so. I can get you them ten apiece."

"How about nine?" Wayne said, negotiating like his rich Wall Street friends. Big Dawg sat back in his chair like he was thinking for a minute.

"A'ight, I'll fuck with y'all. Give me about a month and we'll make it happen. I'll be in touch with Mesha to let you know what's going on."

"A month is a long time," J Mo said.

"If you want A-1 shit for a cheap price, then a month. If you want some bullshit, then I can make it happen in a week. It's whatever with me, but the price ain't gonna change."

"A month is cool. It's been a pleasure doing business with you," J Mo replied, knowing they could cut A-1 cocaine a few times before they even sold it and made millions.

J Mo and Wayne got up from their seats and shook Big Dawg's hand again. "Y'all mind if I steal Mesha for a minute? I'm going to send her right out."

"No problem. We'll be in the car, baby."

"Okay," Mesha said before smooching Wayne on the lips on the way out. Big Dawg waited a few minutes before speaking.

"Bitch, do you want me to kill this nigga?" he said, putting his nickel-plated .45 automatic on the desk.

"Daddy, be cool. It's almost over. You know I gotta make this shit look real. I know you want this money, don't you?"

"Yeah, boo. I'm just saying, I ain't about no nigga kissing you in front of me and shit. I'm already putting up with this clown."

"Quit acting crazy, daddy. You know this pussy is all yours. That smooch is as close as he'll ever get to this pussy," Mesha said, sitting on Big Dawg's lap like he was Santa Claus before kissing him on his cheek and rubbing his big belly, knowing she had sat that pussy on Wayne's face right before she came there.

"You know I be getting jealous and shit, boo."

"It's okay, daddy. Let me catch them before they start

thinking something."

"Okay, let me walk you out," he said, slapping Mesha across her phat ass as she got up.

"I'll call you."

"A'ight," Big Dawg said as they walked out of the office and to the front of the Laundromat. Big Dawg was watching her phat ass as she walked out of the shop.

"You good, boss?" asked one of Big Dawg's goons who was standing outside his office.

"I'm gon' fuck around and have to kill all these muthafuckas," Big Dawg replied, lighting his Newport.

***

"Everything good, sweetheart?" Wayne asked as Mesha got in the back of the black Suburban.

"Everything is fine. He looking forward to doing business with y'all."

"Good, I'm ready to get this show on the road," Wayne said before his brother, J Mo, pulled off from the curb. The ride was quiet until they pulled up at the Aloft Hotel that they were staying at.

"Aye, Mesha, you go order everyone some food. Me and Wayne will be right back," J Mo said, handing Mesha a hundred-dollar bill over his shoulder.

"I guess," Mesha said with an attitude, feeling like she was getting paid to get out of the truck. As soon as the door closed, J Mo pulled off.

"What's the deal, bro?"

"Nigga, I don't trust this bitch."

"I'm telling you, she good. She ain't the fucking police or nothing."

"Nigga, I ain't talking about the police. That bitch sleeping with her best friend's husband. What happens if Tay Tay find out? Nigga, that's a problem we don't need. This is one of the biggest deals we've ever had. Our careers are on the line, and I ain't about to let no Jerry Springer shit fuck it up," J Mo said, knowing his brother.

"Just 'cause you a couple of years older than me don't mean you always know what the fuck you're talking about. For your information, I'm leaving Taylor, and I'm going to be with Mesha when I do."

"Leaving? Nigga, you ain't get no prenup. She gon' leave with half of everything."

"Not if she's dead!" Wayne said, making them both stop talking.

***

It had been two days since Sa'vere had heard from Tay Tay. And when she contacted him, all she told him was an address. His brown box Chevy didn't fit in the high-class neighborhood in Arlington Heights. Pulling into the long driveway, Sa'vere never would've imagined the mansion that was hidden behind the trees.

"Damn!" he said seeing the house. Just as the words left his lips, his cell phone rang. "What's good, Tay? I just pulled up to this address you gave me. This crib is crazy."

"Well, I'm happy you like it because it's your new place. I told you I can't have my nigga in no run-down hotel."

"Damn, boo, thanks. I told you I'm from the trap. That's my life."

"And I told you this is your new crib."

"Well, I ain't going to argue with you," he said, seeing the all-white Porsche Panamera parked in the open garage.

"I got you a gift too, and this ain't even up for debate or argument."

"A'ight, boo."

"I'm happy we have an understanding. That Porsche in the garage is yours. Go ahead and make yourself at home. I'll call you later. I love you."

"I love you too, Tay," Sa'vere said before hanging up. Sa'vere turned off his car and just sat there for a minute. He had to get his thoughts together, especially with these feelings he had been having for Tay Tay. The words "I love you" were becoming easier and easier for him, and when he said it to her, it felt different.

"Oh, well, welcome home, nigga. I just might be in love," Sa'vere said to himself, thinking out loud as he got out of the car, ready to check out the inside.

Sa'vere walked through the unlocked front door and inside the house. He was blown away by what he was seeing. The mansion should've been on *MTV Cribs*, Sa'vere thought to himself, looking around. He looked on the table next to the door, and there was a note with a Porsche key, house key, and five stacks of money with ten thousand-dollar money bands wrapped around them. He smiled as he picked up the letter and began reading it.

Dear luv, I don't know where you came from, but I'm happy you're here. Call this an investment in our future.

See you soon. I love you, Tay.

Sa'vere was shaking his head as he put the letter back down. He was about to go check out the pond that he could see through the huge windows that covered the back of the house, but his phone ringing stopped him.

"What up, Trell?"

"Nigga, we supposed to be meeting. Where you at?"

"Damn, my bad. I lost track of time. Give me about thirty minutes, maybe twenty. I'm en route now," Sa'vere said, grabbing the Porsche key and three stacks of money after hanging up the phone.

***

When Sa'vere pulled up at the Motel 6, Mesha and Trell were sitting in the parking lot outside Sa'vere's room.

"Well, look at this nigga!" Trell said, smoking his cigarette as Sa'vere got out of the white Porsche.

"Damn, you must got Tay Tay wide open," Mesha said, following Sa'vere into the room.

"Nigga, you riding around in Porsches and shit. When this shit gon' pay off for us?"

"Shut up, nigga," Sa'vere said, pulling the three stacks of money out of his back pockets. He immediately threw one to Trell, then another to Mesha.

"*That's* what's I'm talking about. My nigga always come through."

"Then why you always talking shit?"

"'Cause, that's what I do, nigga."

"Well, Mesha, I can't lie. You were right. This is our biggest payout. I'm about to cut this bitch off."

"Fuck that, baby. You gon' have to play your part a little bit longer. I just put together something so big, this could have us all set for life."

"What's going on?"

"I plugged Wayne with Big Dawg, and it's about to be millions on the table."

"What we gon' do, rob them?" Trell asked, always thirsty for some money.

"That could definitely be an option, but right now, we need to just do what we been doing until we figure out the next move," Mesha said, lighting her blunt.

"We can hit this lick without Tay Tay involved."

"Fuck that bitch, nigga. Did you hear her say, *millions* on the table?" Trell said.

"Nigga, you getting soft on me for Tay Tay. Don't fucking play with me, Sa'vere. I swear to God, I'll kill that bitch myself," Mesha said, getting pissed.

"Be the fuck cool. I'm just saying, if we gonna hit a lick like that, we need the least amount of people involved. She's just an extra witness."

"Well, in the meantime, she just gonna have to be a fucking witness. Come here," Sa'vere said, grabbing Mesha by her arm.

"What, nigga?"

"Quit acting crazy. You know I got this. I'm just looking out for our safety too."

"You get on my damn nerves."

"I know," Sa'vere said, pulling her close as she poked her lips out, pouting.

"Move."

"I ain't. Let's go spend some of this money."

"See, you know all the right things to say, boo," Mesha said, smiling.

"Well, let's do something. This love shit making me sick," Trell said, opening the room door and heading outside.

***

The shopping spree was what they all needed to cool off. Sa'vere spoiled Mesha and made sure he put a smile on her face. He was trying to take her attention off of Tay Tay, and he knew that shopping and some dick would do just that. Mesha had told them she had business to handle, so they dropped her off. Sa'vere had been wanting to kick it with his boy anyway.

"Nigga, what's really going on?"

"Shit," Sa'vere replied as he drove, not trying to look over at Trell who was staring upside his head.

"Nigga, quit playing. I been your ace forever. I know when you feeling a female, and Tay Tay got you feeling something. Shit, if a bitch put me in a Porsche, I'd have some feelings too."

"A house too," Sa'vere said, still not looking at his friend.

"A house? Nigga, get the fuck out of here!"

"Yeah, I'm lying. She ain't get me no house; she got me a mansion."

"Nigga, quit stunting."

Sa'vere didn't say anything; he just laughed as he jumped on the highway exit to Arlington Heights. Trell sat back in his seat and lit the Backwoods blunt full of loud, enjoying the ride.

***

Trell couldn't believe the mansion Sa'vere was living in. Sa'vere even gave Trell another $10,000.

"Nigga, this place got a pond and shit like a damn castle or something. I sure appreciate the bread, bruh."

"Nigga, you know it's all love. I eat, you eat. That's how it's always been."

"No doubt," Trell replied, giving Sa'vere some dap.

"This little money ain't shit. It's plenty more if we play our cards right. Mesha gon' have us doing life somewhere. She's way too thirsty."

"You know I'm with you 100 percent. What's the plan?"

"I don't know yet, but this mansion and that extra bread stays between us. I'm going to come up with a plan, trust me."

"Nigga, what the fuck I look like saying something. You know you be saying some crazy shit sometimes."

"Nigga, I'm just saying. I know one thing for sure . . . We gotta get far away from Mesha's crazy ass. Nigga, look around. We can live like bosses and say fuck that bitch."

"Well, in that case, point me to the bar and let's drink to success."

"Shit, nigga, I don't even know where it's at," Sa'vere said, making them both laugh. Sa'vere knew it was time to shake Mesha and move on to better things, which was Tay Tay. He knew that no matter how much money they came up with, Mesha would never be satisfied. So as long as there was a dollar to be made, she didn't care what she had to do to get it. He almost regretted meeting Mesha, but he couldn't blame nobody but himself. He knew she was with Big Dawg and saw her as a quick fuck and a couple of dollars, but he got in way too deep with her, not knowing how thirsty and cutthroat she was. At first, he saw a check, but now he was thinking all money wasn't good money, especially if it had Mesha's hands on it. He and Trell had been grinding way too long to go out like some suckas, he thought, while trying to go find his new bar.

Chapter 4

Tired of Being Sick and Tired

The next two weeks had been crazy for Tay Tay and Wayne. The love in the house had been colder than a polar bear's toenail. Tay Tay had even been sleeping in her office and enjoying it, but it was only a matter of time before things boiled over.

"Taylor, where the fuck is my tie at? I'm going to miss my damn flight."

"I don't wear ties. Ask one of your bitches. I'm tired of being your wife when it's convenient. I'm sure there's plenty of men dying to have a good woman like me on their team," Tay Tay said.

"You know what, Taylor? You're one of the smartest stupid bitches I know. You need to watch your fucking mouth." Wayne said a lot of things, but he had never called Tay Tay a bitch before, and the word triggered another side of her.

"*You* the bitch!" she said before spitting in his face. Tay Tay didn't know what to expect, but the answer came fast.

Before she could blink, Wayne had slapped her and began choking her.

"Bitch, you ain't shit without me! *I* made you who you are and don't you fucking forget it. *I'm* the reason you're allowed to keep breathing right now," Wayne said, throwing her to the floor. Tay Tay rubbed her throat as she gasped for air.

"Fuck you, bitch. You don't scare me!"

"You still talking?" Wayne said, approaching her. Tay Tay jumped to her feet, and as soon as Wayne grabbed her, she clawed his cheek with her hundred-dollar manicure, then hit him in his nose with her fist. Wayne was in shock that she hit him, but he quickly shook it off and didn't hold anything back as he swung a vicious right hand that hit her in her jaw. The blow left a cracking sound echoing in the air, and it knocked her to the floor. Before she could recover from the blow, Wayne grabbed her by her red hair and dragged her to the bed.

"Bitch, you are *my* fucking property, and it's time you learned it!" he said, pushing her facedown in the bed as he pulled his dick out. Tay Tay was dizzy from the blow but was trying to fight back. Wayne laughed as he spit in his hand and rubbed it on his dick for lubrication.

"Fuck you!" Tay Tay said, spitting blood on the bed as he snatched her pajama pants down.

"No, fuck you, bitch!" he said as he rammed his dick in her phat ass. Tay Tay tried to scream, but he pushed her face in the bed like he was suffocating her. Wayne showed no mercy and the more pain she seemed to be in, the more turned on he was. Tay Tay could feel herself being ripped open as he continued to pound in her ass, but her suffocating had her too weak to fight back. She felt herself passing out, but his hot load shooting in her ass gave her the relief she needed to breathe. All she could do was fall to the floor on all fours, trying to suck in some air after he pulled his dick out of her bleeding ass.

"You do what the fuck I tell *you*, and you better not fucking forget that shit, bitch!" Wayne said, kicking her in her side like he would a dude. Tay Tay felt the rest of the air she had left in her body leave her, and excruciating pain in her ribs consumed her as she fell over on her other side.

"Now, next time *I* tell you to find my fucking tie, fucking do it, bitch!"

Tay Tay could barely hear his words as she tried to remain conscious. She looked over at him with her vision blurry and couldn't make out what he was doing until she felt hot liquid spraying on her and the strong smell of urine filled her nostrils. The last thing she saw was Wayne shaking his dick off like he was standing over the toilet. She had taken many beatings from him over the years, but this was the first time she fought back. She smiled to herself before passing out.

***

When the hospital called Sa'vere and told him that his wife Taylor had been in an accident, he didn't know what to think. He just jumped in the Porsche and headed to the hospital in Waukegan. When he walked in the room, there she was sitting on the edge of the bed. She turned around as she heard him come in, and he could see her cheek was swollen. Tears instantly began running down her face. Sa'vere had to hold back his own tears as he went to her. He could see she was in pain as she lifted her arms. Sa'vere just hugged her, and she rested her head on his chest. He kissed the top of her head as a tear ran down his cheek and onto her hair as he held her. He knew the doctor saying she had fallen down the stairs was a lie. He had been talking to Tay Tay every time she got a free moment and had been trying to convince her to act normal. Sa'vere knew having another man to run to made a female start acting funny with her man. Then the next thing you know, it's a problem.

"He did this to you, didn't he?" Sa'vere asked, trying to get verification on his theory.

"Yes. I hate him!" Tay Tay said, and she meant it. The whole time she was in the shower before she caught a cab to the hospital, she thought about nothing but killing him.

"Come on, let's get out of here. Where's your car?"

"At home. I caught a cab."

"Where's Wayne?" Sa'vere asked, even though he knew he was probably with Mesha in Dallas.

"In the air somewhere. He won't be back for a few days."

"I bet," Sa'vere said under his breath ready to fuck Wayne up. The nurse came in and brought the wheelchair. Sa'vere picked her up off the bed like he was carrying her across the threshold.

"We don't need that. I got this," he said, carrying Tay Tay past her. Tay Tay just lay her head on his chest, feeling safe in his arms.

"I love you."

"I love you too, Tay Tay," Sa'vere said as he carried her into the hallway. He didn't care if she was right or wrong. All he knew was Wayne was going to pay when he got his hands on him.

The ride to the mansion took them over an hour, and Tay Tay slept most of it. The king-size bed in the mansion had Tay Tay's name written all over it, and she didn't hesitate to strip down naked and get in the bed when they arrived. Sa'vere sat on the side of the bed drinking from the fifth of Hennessey. He was looking out at the rain running down the window. He had so many different emotions going on inside him, and he was hoping each shot of Hennessey numbed them, but he knew he had too many wounds in his life to heal them all. He felt like what happened to Tay Tay was his fault, and he didn't know what to do to fix it. He had never known love his whole life because what he thought was love with Mesha was nothing like the feelings he felt for Tay Tay. He wanted to tell her the truth about everything, but he knew there was a chance he could lose her, and now wasn't the time to risk that. He owed it to her to think of a plan.

Looking over his shoulder at Tay Tay as he drank from his bottle, she looked so precious to him, and he planned on protecting her at all costs, even if he had to put his life on the line. He finally felt his inner savage coming alive.

***

"Damn, what happened to you?" Mesha asked, looking at the scratches on Wayne's face as he let her into his downtown Dallas hotel room.

"Your crazy-ass friend, *that's* what happened. I'm tired of that bitch," Wayne said, closing the door behind her.

"Awww, daddy, I told you that bitch don't know how to treat a boss nigga like you," Mesha said, rubbing his rock-hard dick through his suit pants.

"You damn right about that. You the only female that understands me."

"You know what I need, daddy?"

"What?" he replied as she kept rubbing his dick.

"I want to be your wife. I'm tired of this bitch in my position. She living good with new cars and shit, and I ain't got nothing but a damn hotel room. I should walk up out of here," Mesha said, turning around and heading over to the room door.

"Wait, Mesha, baby. I want you to be my wife. Tell me what kind of car you want and it's yours. I wish I could marry you right now, but this bitch is in the way."

"Well, we gotta figure something out soon, 'cause I'm tired of playing second to this bitch."

"I swear I'm on it, baby."

"What the fuck you call me?" Mesha said, poking him in his chest.

"I'm sorry."

"You're not fucking sorry. Now get down on your fucking knees, you little lying bitch," Mesha said with a straight face.

"Yes, mama. I'm so sorry."

"Oh, you want to keep fucking talking. Well, I got something for bitches that keep talking," Mesha said before pulling her little black dress up with one hand and her matching panties to the side.

"Please, I'm so sorry, I won't do it again, mama."

"I know you won't, now shut up and eat, little bitch," Mesha said, grabbing his head and pulling it to her pussy, forcing Wayne to eat her out. Mesha smiled knowing she had her meal ticket on his knees being her bitch. It was only a matter of time before she was Ms. Wayne Washington, she thought to herself, trying to make him drown in her pussy.

***

Wayne was up before the sun came up, and even after being Mesha's sex slave for most of the night, his mind wouldn't let him rest. "Wayne, lay your ass down."

"I can't. You right. I need to treat you better. When the car lot opens, we going to get you anything you want. I'd leave Taylor today, but she would get half of everything, and I'll be damned if this bitch walks away with a dime of my money."

"Wayne, calm down. That bitch ain't gonna get a dime. I can promise you that. You need to focus on this big deal coming up and getting this money. Let your wifey handle the small things, daddy."

"Now see, that's why I love you."

"I love you too, daddy, now come back to bed and get some of your pussy," Mesha said, throwing the blanket off her naked body.

Wayne jumped right in the bed and into that pussy. His hump game was weak as usual, so Mesha grabbed his ass with her hands and pulled him balls deep into her pussy.

"Shit, Mesha!"

"Damn, Wayne, you killing this pussy," she responded, stroking his ego. She was tired and really wanted to go back to sleep so she made her pussy grip his dick and suck the nut out of it like a vacuum cleaner.

"You coming, mama?"

"Yes, you big dick muthafucka," she said, shaking like she was coming.

"That's right; don't play with this dick," he said, rolling out of the pussy.

"Ooh, daddy, I swear I won't," Mesha said rolling over, trying not to laugh at him.

***

The next few days, Sa'vere spent taking care of Tay Tay from bathing her to feeding her. She had never been cherished like this before, and as she watched Sa'vere sleep next to her in his boxers, she felt like she needed to show him some appreciation. As soon as she touched his dick, it became rock hard. She pulled it out of the boxer opening and stroked it a couple of times before climbing on top of it. Her ribs were bruised, but she didn't care about the pain. She wanted that dick, and she was going to get it. She could barely sit all the way down on his dick and tried to take it slow, but Sa'vere pushed upward, giving her no choice but to get it all.

"Damn damn damn!" Tay Tay said in pleasure as she grinded her thick hips all over that dick. Sa'vere grabbed her big titties and squeezed them together as she continued to ride his dick until she had come running out of her pussy down to his balls. Tay Tay put her knees in front of her while staying on top of the dick, then put her hands on her knees and went to work squatting all over that dick. She felt Sa'vere's dick throbbing, ready to bust all inside her, so she dropped that pussy up and down his dick like a pogo stick until come splashed all inside her.

"Shit, bitch!"

"That's right, nigga, give me that shit," Tay Tay said right before she found herself coming hard. She put her knees back down on the bed and leaned forward. He pulled her close, and they kissed. Before they both knew it, they fell asleep.

The next two weeks had been quiet at Tay Tay's home. They avoided each other as much as they could when Wayne was in town. Tay Tay stayed on the phone with Sa'vere every chance she got. When Wayne was away, she was either meeting Sa'vere or talking to him on the phone until they both fell asleep like teenagers. Those phone calls were the only thing that stopped Tay Tay from putting a bullet in Wayne's head. Sa'vere had told her to be cool and act like everything was fine until they figured out a plan. Tay Tay was happy Wayne was gone when Mesha called to see if she and Sa'vere wanted to come out to party with her at Club Roxy. Tay Tay definitely wanted the opportunity to hang out with her new lover and to talk to the club owner about what happened to her girl, Stacey.

Club Roxy was packed like the last time Tay Tay went there with Mesha. But unlike the last time, Mesha seemed to have a new stream of wealth. The bottles kept coming, and they kept drinking.

Sa'vere was feeling some type of way because he had been avoiding Mesha and didn't want Tay Tay around her. Despite how he felt, the only thing he could do was act like he was enjoying himself for Tay Tay's sake. He could tell by the look on Mesha's face that she had some words for him, and he planned on avoiding them at all costs.

"Shit, we turned up in this bitch tonight. I'll be back in a minute. Y'all lovebirds going to be okay?" Mesha said, passing Tay Tay the bottle of Hennessey that she had in her hand.

"Girl, bye. Me and my boo good. You need to be trying to find you a boo in here and stop worrying about me."

"Trust me, bitch, I can have a boo whenever I want one," Mesha replied with a smile before walking off.

"Whatever. She always talking shit. You good, boo? You been a little quiet tonight," Tay Tay said, sitting on Sa'vere's lap and passing him the bottle.

"I'm good, baby. Sometimes I get so caught up in thinking how lucky I am to have you in my life. You were right; you did change my life, and I love you for that." Sa'vere didn't know when the truth was going to come out, especially dealing with Mesha, so he was going to do his best to show Tay Tay he wasn't the same nigga she met in the beginning. Hopefully, she would know his love was true.

"Damn, Sa'vere, I love you too. Nigga, you gon' have me crying up in here and shit," she said before kissing him softly on his lips.

"Is that my sister?"

Tay Tay glanced behind Sa'vere. "Oh shit, Snoop, what you doing here?"

"You know I'm chasing them thots, sis."

"You crazy. There's someone I want you to meet. Sa'vere, this my twin brother, Snoop."

"What's good, fam?" Sa'vere said, getting up and shaking Snoop's hand.

"Good to meet you, bruh."

"Sa'vere just might be your brother-in-law," Tay Tay said, knowing she hadn't told her brother about Wayne because he'd end up with a life sentence.

"Well, welcome to the family, bruh," Snoop said, holding his Rémy bottle up and toasting with Sa'vere.

"You in here all fresh and shit," Tay Tay said, checking out her brother's new Pelle Pelle outfit.

"Well, when you got a ballin'-ass sister, what can you do but stay fresh?" Snoop said, hugging his sister.

"Well, I can't argue with that," Tay Tay said, all smiles at being with her two favorite men in the world.

"Was that Mesha's thick ass I seen up here?"

"There you go. Yeah, that was Mesha."

"Where she go, 'cause a nigga trying to say hi."

"Whatever, fool. Shit, you might as well take a seat. She should be back in a minute," Tay Tay said, drinking from her glass.

The next fifteen minutes they spent drinking and joking. Then Snoop spotted who he was looking for.

"There go that nigga, Ted, right there. You want to holler at him?" Snoop asked, recognizing Ted even though he hadn't seen him in five years.

"Hell, yeah," Tay Tay said, getting up off Sa'vere's lap. "Come on, sis."

"We'll be right back. Tell Mesha to sit tight when she gets back, I got somebody who wants to meet her."

"A'ight," Sa'vere said, knowing damn well Mesha didn't need to get up with Tay Tay's brother. He didn't wish Mesha on no man, not even his enemy. Tay Tay didn't say anything else. She just walked off, following her brother through the club. She couldn't help but wonder where Mesha was, not knowing Mesha had been watching her the whole time.

***

"I told you she was cheating. The only way you gonna get the plugs your brother got is for me to be on the inside, and the only way that's gonna happen is with her out of the way."

"Yeah, you right. I think I might have an idea," J Mo said, drinking his glass of Crown Royal.

"I knew you would come up with something, daddy."

"That's because I'm the real brains of this operation. Wayne's lame ass wouldn't be shit without me," J Mo said, knowing the only reason Wayne was getting more money than him was because of his rich Wall Street buddies.

"You damn right, daddy! Damn, you make my pussy wet when you talk like that."

"Well, I got some more talk for you later on tonight, so answer your phone when I call you. I'm about to get out of here before Tay Tay sees me."

"I will, baby. I'm looking forward to it because the last time we were in Dallas, you had me coming everywhere, daddy," Mesha said, whispering in his ear.

"Yeah, that shit was epic. Oh yeah, one more thing. What's that nigga's name she's with? I don't give a fuck how lame my brother is, that nigga gotta pay."

"Sa'vere."

"Fasho. That nigga gon' wish he found himself another bitch when I'm through with him," J Mo said, finishing his glass of Crown Royal before walking off. Mesha just stood there for a second with a devilish grin on her face, loving her dirty work, before heading back to Tay Tay and Sa'vere.

***

"Ted, what's good, homie? I see you doing big things now," Snoop said as he walked up on Ted and his two goons sitting at their table.

"You look familiar."

"Nigga, it's me, Snoop."

"Damn, nigga, what's good? When you get out?"

"A few weeks ago."

"*That's* what's up. Happy you could come out," said a heavyset, brown-skinned girl with gold Versace glasses.

"No doubt. This is my sister, Tay Tay. She wanted to holler at you about something."

"I wanted to know what happened to Stacey."

"Stacey?"

"Yeah, Stacey."

"That's why your name sounds familiar. You the one

they call 'College girl.'"

"Yeah, that's me," Tay Tay said. She hadn't heard the nickname Mesha and Stacey had given her since college.

"That shit was unfortunate, that's all I know."

"*Unfortunate*, nigga? Damn, you better show my girl some respect."

"Come on, Tay Tay. He didn't mean it like that."

"Oh, I mean it like that. I'm taking care of this bitch, and come to find out, she had been stealing from me. When the police found that bitch, she was filled with bullets and had five kilos in the trunk."

"Nigga, fuck you and your dope!" Tay Tay said, letting the liquor speak for her.

"Everything okay?" Sa'vere asked, walking up.

"Bitch, this my club. Fam, you better get your sister 'for her mouth get her in trouble," Ted said, standing up.

"Get her, nigga? Who gon' get me, though?" Snoop said before swinging and hitting Ted in his eye, smashing his $400 glasses. One of Ted's goons tried to swing on Snoop, but Sa'vere gave him a two-piece that sent him crashing into the table. Blows were flying everywhere as the club went up in a panic. Snoop and Sa'vere were going crazy on Ted and his goons, and Tay Tay couldn't help but hit Ted with a bottle, splitting his head open. By the time security got to them, Sa'vere and Snoop were beating the other goon Ted had with him under one of the tables while Ted and the other goon were bloody and almost unconscious. Tay Tay knew her brother was crazy, but seeing Sa'vere was just as crazy, she knew he was going to fit right in with the family.

***

Tay Tay hated being at home, especially when Wayne was there. Hearing his expensive designer shoes coming toward the kitchen, she dreaded the moment he entered the room. She focused on eating her breakfast.

"Taylor," Wayne said, but Tay Tay kept eating her cheese eggs, ignoring him.

"Taylor, I'm sorry for what I did to you. You didn't deserve that. I let my frustrations over the business get the best of me. I promise it'll never happen again. I've been hard on you when I should have been spoiling you for helping me build this empire. There's a big deal coming up next week, so I think you should go spend time with your friends and family, my treat." Tay Tay dropped her fork and looked over at Wayne. She couldn't believe what he was saying. If this was his way of making up, she sure was about to take advantage of it.

"I guess so, Wayne."

"I know I've apologized before, but this time is different. I think you being around your family and friends is a good thing. Trust me, it will never happen again. Here, I bought you something," Wayne finished saying, sliding over a key to a Bentley coupe.

"We'll see," Tay Tay said, like she was forgiving him, even though she was waaay past forgiveness. He was lucky she wasn't stabbing him with her breakfast fork, she thought to herself, giving him a smile before he walked away. She hated him, but she sure wasn't about to turn down a free Bentley.

***

Tay Tay packed her bags for her week getaway. She couldn't wait until it was permanent. She locked the house and walked outside to her new white-on-white Bentley coupe sitting in the driveway. She put her bags in the back and got in. She looked in the passenger seat and there was a big yellow envelope. She looked inside, and there were seven stacks of money with $10,000 money bands wrapped around them. She pulled out her phone and dialed the number that said "Auntie."

"Sa'vere, I'm on my way, baby," Tay Tay said, looking in the mirror making sure her lip gloss was popping because her lips were yearning to be on Sa'vere's.

The next couple of days, Tay Tay spent with Sa'vere at their mansion hideaway having sex like two teenagers just discovering pleasure. When they weren't fucking, they were shopping and enjoying the finer things Chicago had to offer.

Tay Tay wanted to take Sa'vere to meet the rest of her family, so she planned a barbecue at her mother's house. Sa'vere was accepted right away, especially since Snoop had been bragging to his mother about how he and Sa'vere had put their hands on Ted and his goons for talking crazy to Tay Tay. Tay Tay was smiling on the inside and out for the first time in a long time. When she thought of marriage, *this* was the image she had always pictured for herself. She sipped on her Watermelon Rita while watching Sa'vere and Snoop play spades against her mother and her aunt, Stella, who was her mother's twin. Everything seemed perfect . . . until Alisha came out the back door.

"Oh my God, since this bitch came back around, now it's a damn party and shit."

"Alisha!" Ms. Brown yelled, trying to calm the situation down.

"I ain't about to bite my tongue like she all that or something."

"First off, bitch, you need to watch who you talking to. I done let you vent last time I seen you, but this time ain't gon' be the same," Tay Tay said, sitting her can down and getting up out of her chair, adjusting her sundress.

"Fuck you, bitch, you ain't shit!"

Alisha could barely get the last word out of her mouth before Tay Tay was on her ass. Ms. Brown smiled knowing she was only trying to calm the situation down so Tay Tay wouldn't hurt her. Alisha tried to fight back, but her sister was like a savage, and before she knew it, Tay Tay was sitting on her, hitting her in her face.

"Bitch, don't *ever* talk to me like you crazy!" Tay Tay yelled as Snoop and Sa'vere pulled her off of Alisha.

"I hate you!" Alisha screamed while crying with a bloody mouth.

"You ain't gotta love me, but best believe, you gon' respect me, bitch!" Tay Tay replied while being held back from round two. Alisha got up and ran in the house as Aunt Stella followed trying not to laugh.

Sa'vere couldn't do anything but shake his head, loving the feeling of family, even though it had just gone down. After his mom died when he was seventeen, the only family he really had was his best friend, Trell, his older sister, Pam, and whatever lady he laid up with. He was amazed at the feeling he was having. Tay Tay was changing his life day by day, and he was happy she was his. He hugged her tighter, still trying to calm her down.

"Come on, boo, be easy; it's over," he said softly in her ear. His words sent a chill down her spine and calmed her like she had just gotten a massage.

"You damn right, calm down. I been gone five years, and we gon' eat some muthafuckin' barbecue. Alisha, I'm gon' eat yours 'cause that lip big than a muthafucka!" Snoop yelled.

"Shut up, fool, 'for you get some too," Tay Tay said, hitting him playfully.

"This my jam. Y'all bring y'all's asses on and let's party! Sa'vere, get over here and come have a drink with your mother-in-law," Ms. Brown said, hearing "How Do You Want It" by 2Pac and Jodeci.

"Okay, Mama, don't be trying to take my man."

"Girl, shut up. Where you think you got your moves from?" Ms. Brown said, making them all laugh as she continued dancing while pouring drinks.

***

When Mesha called Tay Tay and said she wanted to go to lunch and do some shopping with her, Tay Tay couldn't wait. She felt like she owed her girl, and she was going to do everything in her power to prove it. After shopping downtown Chicago, they decided to go to Goose Island for some shrimp. They ate until they were full and were ready to do some more shopping.

"Damn, girl, you go ahead to the car. I gotta use the

bathroom right fast," Mesha said as they came out of the restaurant.

"Okay, I'll pull the car around," Tay Tay replied as Mesha walked back in the restaurant. Tay Tay got to her car when she heard fast approaching footsteps.

"Freeze, police!" one of the plainclothes officers yelled, approaching her with guns drawn.

"What the fuck is going on?" Tay Tay said, dropping her leftovers and Louis Vuitton purse on the ground.

"Get on the ground!" the officer yelled, slamming her to the ground and cuffing her.

"I ain't did shit!"

The dark-haired, middle-aged white man didn't reply. He just whistled for the dog. Tay Tay didn't know what was going on as she lay on the ground watching the officer begin running the K-9 around the car.

The dog got to the front of the car and went crazy. The officer that had cuffed her walked over to the car where the dog and the other officer were standing. He kneeled down and reached under the bumper like he knew something was there. He pulled his knife from his pocket and stuck it under the bumper. Tay Tay couldn't do anything but watch as the officer stuck the knife under it and a stream of white powder came pouring out like sand from an hourglass.

"This car's brand new!" Tay Tay yelled.

"Shut the fuck up. You're under arrest for possession and intent to deliver. Get her in a fucking squad car!" the officer yelled.

"I swear I don't know what the fuck is going on," Tay Tay said, getting dragged away.

Mesha was watching from the restaurant window like the other people trying to see what was going on. She pulled her phone out of her purse and dialed a number.

"What, Mesha? I said this shit's over!" Sa'vere said.

"You damn right, it's over, nigga. For you and that bitch! Nigga, you thought you could play me for her and run off living happily ever after, nigga? You got me fucked up. I'm about to send you a video, nigga. Have a great fucking life," Mesha said before hanging up in his face.

Sa'vere was ready to start going in on Mesha, but realized the phone call was over. He looked down at his phone screen and a video message started coming in. Sa'vere pushed PLAY as soon as the video loaded. Anger and hurt instantly filled every inch of his body as he watched Tay Tay being slammed to the ground and arrested.

"Fuuuuuuuuck!" he yelled before slapping his fifth of Hennessey on the floor. He knew one day this game would come back to bite him, and today was that day. He grabbed his shirt and car keys and headed out.

*****

Tay Tay hadn't been in jail since she was a juvenile for retail theft with her girls, Mesha and Stacey. She had only been at the station for a few hours, but this time, she had spent the night. She couldn't sleep, especially since she still didn't know why she was in jail.

She was ready for court like the rest of the females in the smelly bullpen and was finally called out. She didn't know where the sheriff was taking her until she arrived at a room door. The sheriff pressed a button next to the door before it opened. He opened the door, and she could see the white officer that arrested her sitting at a table.

"Well, if it isn't the drug queen-pin. Come on in and have a seat. I'm Detective Conan, and I'm with the drug and gang task force."

"I don't know what's going on."

"So, you're telling me you don't know anything about the ten kilos of cocaine in your bumper?"

"Hell, naw, that car's brand new."

"I don't give a fuck how old it is. Right now, you're facing a lot of time. I'm talking about a life sentence. Only thing you can do now is help yourself. I need to know where the dope came from and who you work for."

"I don't know! I swear."

"You can play all the games you want, but you're going down for a long time!" Detective Conan said, slamming his hand on the table before walking out. Tay Tay wanted to put this all on Wayne, but snitching wasn't in her blood.

The courtroom was packed, but Tay Tay saw Sa'vere when she was walked in the courtroom by the deputies.

Everything felt unreal to her. She thought her attorney was supposed to be there, but he was a no-show. Tay Tay almost didn't hear the judge calling her name.

"What is the bond recommendation?"

"Ms. Washington was found with ten kilos of cocaine in her bumper. She has a visa and money to travel. The state requests bail be set at $2 million."

"Two million? I don't even know what's going on."

"Well, ma'am, I suggest you get a lawyer and find out.

Bond is set at $2 million upon release. Passport is to be surrendered," the judge said before slamming his gavel down. Tay Tay couldn't believe what he had just said. She wasn't worried, though. A few phone calls, and she would be out, she thought to herself, trying not to let Sa'vere see her cry as she was escorted out of the courtroom.

Tay Tay spent the rest of her day trying to call Wayne, but she wasn't getting a response. By the time she was taken to general population, it was nighttime. She finally remembered Sa'vere's number, especially since she wasn't used to seeing it. She dialed the number, and the operator put her on hold. She waited for what felt like forever, praying that he accepted the call. All her calls to Wayne just eventually hung up on her.

"Your call has been accepted."

"Tay Tay, are you okay, baby?"

"Yeah, I'm okay. Sa'vere, I don't know what the fuck is going on. Somebody set me up," Tay Tay said.

"Well, what you want me to do?"

"I got enough money to bail out, but I can't do nothing until tomorrow. You might have to make some calls for me."

"It's whatever, boo, I gotcha. I been waiting on you to call all day."

"They done had me where I couldn't talk on the phone. When they did give me a call, the lawyer wouldn't answer."

"That's fucked up. The judge's bitch ass said two million. I'm like what the fuck is going on? I sure ain't got no two million, baby, but you can have my last penny to help. At the end of the day, you better know I'll do anything to get it."

"I know, boo. I need you to be cool for me. You all I got."

"I gotcha, Tay Tay. I love you, ma."

"I love you too, nigga. I'm about to lay it down and try to sleep this nightmare away."

"Well, I'll meet you in your dreams. It don't matter where we at; nothing can stop our love. You understand?"

"Yeah, I understand."

"Naw, tell me nothing can stop our love."

"Nothing can stop our love, Sa'vere."

"Now that's better. Call whenever. I'm here."

"Okay, I love you."

"Love you too," Sa'vere said, hanging up the phone. Tay Tay just held the phone for a few seconds, wishing she could say those words to his face. She hung up the phone and walked to her holding cell and closed the door behind her.

The night was long, and Tay Tay didn't know if she had been asleep or not. It was right after breakfast, which was a sack lunch that she refused to eat, when the guard called her out to see her lawyer. Tay Tay couldn't wait to see him and get out of there. She sat in a room with two chairs and a table. It only took a few minutes before a dark-haired white man walked into the room with his briefcase in hand.

"Walter, I've been calling you!" Tay Tay said angrily.

Walter was one of Wayne's close friends from school and also their lawyer. He knew all about their business, and he always kept them safe, which was why Tay Tay was really mad.

"I know, Tay Tay, just calm down. These charges you have against you are serious."

"No shit, Walter. All I'm saying is I don't know where this shit came from."

"Me either, but that's neither here nor there. We need to talk about getting you out of here."

"Good, 'cause I'm tired of being in here. How long until Wayne bails me out?"

"That's all up to you."

"What do you mean?" Tay Tay asked as Walter opened his briefcase and pulled out a folder.

"What is this shit, Walter? I don't have time to be going through these papers and shit. I'm trying to get home and take a shower."

"Well, these papers are divorce papers as well as the release of ownership to any properties and businesses acquired during the marriage."

"Is this some kind of joke you and Wayne are playing, Walter, because I don't think this shit is funny at all?"

"It's far from a joke."

"I don't need him or his money. I got money in my accounts."

"Unfortunately, they seized all of your accounts."

"What the fuck?"

"What Wayne is willing to do for you is bond you out as well as give you a $500,000 compensation. In return, you sign these papers."

"Fuck you and them papers, Walter. He wants to walk away, then I'm going to get my half."

"After the judge sees these photos, I guarantee you'll be walking away with nothing at all," Walter said, pulling some photos out of his briefcase and sliding the stack across the table. Tay Tay couldn't believe what she was seeing. There were pictures of her and Sa'vere. Some were while they were out together like someone had been following them. In others, it was just her. And there were even photos of the two of them inside her Bentley as if taken from a dash cam.

"That dirty muthafucka set me up! I should've known he was playing me. You know what, Walter? You can take all this shit and shove it up your ass, and whatever don't fit, shove it up Wayne's ass. If he thinks he's gonna get away with setting me up, he's got another think coming."

"Tay Tay, think logically here. You either walk away with nothing or leave with a few dollars. A lot of females would die for $500,000 and a get-out-jail-free ticket. You're a businesswoman. You know how things go."

"Fuck you, Walter. I'm going to go ahead and call the guard because I'm going to fuck around and catch a body up in here, and then I'll never get out to get your dirty-ass friend back."

"Well, you know the number if you change your mind. I'll be on call 24/7."

"Fuck you!" Tay Tay said as Walter put his stuff in his briefcase as fast as he could. Tay Tay couldn't believe what was happening to her. The guard came in to escort her back to her cell. She was heated and couldn't wait to get on the phone with Sa'vere. She didn't even give him a chance to answer before she started talking.

"This muthafucka set me up!"

"Who?"

"Wayne!"

"What happened?"

"He sent the lawyer down here with divorce papers and pictures of me and you together like they've been following us. But that ain't shit, 'cause he got pictures from inside the car that Wayne gave me, which just so happened to have dope inside of it that I knew nothing about."

"That's fucked up!"

"You damn right that's fucked up. I can't trust nobody."

"Tay Tay, there's something I need to tell you, and I know the only way to do that is to be real, even though there's a chance I might lose you."

"What is it, Sa'vere?"

"I was a professional side nigga."

"And what's that got to do with me?"

"You were my target."

"Your target? What the fuck is going on, Sa'vere?"

"This is all Mesha fault!"

"What does Mesha have to do with this?"

"I started dating Mesha when she was with some baller from Dallas, trying to catch a couple'a dollars. Next thing I know, I'm with her, hustling females for a living. I ain't gon' lie, I was with it at first, but I wanted out after Stacey. But Mesha's crazy ass wouldn't let me."

"Nigga, you losing me right now! So, you're telling me, you messed with my best friend, Mesha, and she put you onto me and my dead friend, Stacey?"

"I swear, I love you, Tay Tay. I never felt this way about

nobody."

"Nigga, you don't love me! I hope you enjoyed every dime because there is no more us and never will be!"

"Please, Tay Tay, you gotta believe me! I love—"

That was all Tay Tay let him get out before hanging up. *Fuck love,* she thought to herself, as she went back to her cell with her mind racing. She held back the tears until she closed the cell door, even though her pain and hurt was almost unbearable.

It was almost nine o'clock at night by the time they moved Tay Tay to general population. She had a still face on as she was escorted into the three-female cell which already had two females in it.

"You're on the bottom bunk!" the guard said before walking off.

"You okay?" said a medium-built white girl in an orange jail uniform from the top bunk.

"I'm good," Tay Tay replied, despite her heart shattering into a million pieces.

"You don't look good to me. My name is Marisol, and this white bitch is Becky," said the pretty Latina from her bunk across from the bunkbeds.

"Trust me, I'm good. My name is Tay Tay."

"Well, welcome to our home," Marisol said, making Tay Tay laugh.

"See, now you smiling. That's what I'm talking about. No matter how bad shit gets, mama, you gotta find a way to smile through it all," Marisol said with her heavy New York accent.

"That's what's up," Tay Tay said, sitting on her lower

bunk.

"So, what you in for?" Marisol asked.

"Drugs."

"What some weed like Becky?"

"Fuck you, Marisol," Becky said, laughing.

"Nah, I'm talking about something like ten bricks," Tay Tay said.

"Oh shit, it's another trap queen in the cell," Becky said, jumping out of her bunk, laughing.

"Don't pay her crazy ass no attention. She always talking shit. Damn, that's some major weight, mama. How much is your bond?"

"Two million."

"Damn. You gon' be here for a while," Marisol said, sitting up on her bunk.

"Nah, I should be bonding out soon."

"Well, damn, it's like that, mama? Shit, that's heavy pesos. Well, anyway, you right on time for dinner. You want to join us?" Marisol asked, walking to the desk in the cell where a big Doritos bag was folded at the top. It was fat like it was full of something as it sat on a towel.

"Might as well enjoy home," Tay Tay said, trying to make the best of her situation. She needed something to eat and keep her mind off of all the betrayal she was going through.

Chapter 5
A Thin Line between Love and Hate

Sa'vere spent the next few days in the mansion, looking at his cell phone while drinking from a fifth of Hennessey. He had empty bottles on the floor and his .45 automatic on the nightstand. He had never felt so low in his life. Playing females over the years had finally gotten him played. He wondered how many females he had left sitting next to a cell phone with a broken heart, just like he was sitting now, waiting on Tay Tay to call back. He had regretted telling her but knew the only way he could be with her was by being real. So long as things were a secret with Mesha, she would always have a blackmail tool, and he wasn't going to let her do that. He had thought he was heartless, but he knew that was untrue. He felt like everything was his fault. The love of his life was in jail hating him, and he was a long way from the two million he needed to get her out. He just shook his head in disappointment as he guzzled from his Hennessey bottle, finishing it off. That was all the liquor he had left from last night and he was ready to get some more. He grabbed his Backwoods blunt full of loud out of the ashtray, lighting it. As soon as he took a hit, the doorbell rang. Sa'vere held the blunt between his lips like a Newport 100 before grabbing his gun off the nightstand and cocking it. Then he put his phone in his pocket.

"Who the fuck is it?" Sa'vere yelled, aiming his gun at the door.

"It's me, nigga. Open the damn door." Sa'vere hadn't heard Trell's voice in a while, and he quickly opened the door.

"Damn, nigga, you looking rough. I been calling you, and you still ain't answered. You lucky I remembered how to get here."

"Nigga, shit went crazy. Tay Tay's in jail. She's been set up."

"Damn, what the fuck happened?" Trell said, taking the blunt Sa'vere was passing.

"I don't know. She went out with Mesha, and the next thing I know, Mesha's calling me talking shit, and Tay Tay's in jail with ten kilos."

"Get the fuck out of here."

"Nigga, I wish."

"What's her bond?"

"Two million."

"Damn, no wonder you looking like this."

"Nah, nigga, I told her about everything."

"Nigga, you did *what*?"

"I told her about Mesha and Stacey."

"Nigga, you tripping. I knew you was getting soft on me."

"I'm through with this game, Trell, and the only way to get right with Tay Tay is to tell the truth."

"Look at Mr. Lover Lover, all in love and shit."

"Well, I didn't come to find you for no soft shit. I thought about what you said about cutting that bitch, Mesha, off. I got a lick outside of her."

"Oh yeah?"

"Yeah, that nigga Ted y'all stomped out at the club."

"What's good with him? When I was messing with Stacey, she didn't speak on him a lot."

"Dude's a major supplier. He's using that club for a front. He's got several stash houses, but I think one of them is loaded."

"And how do you know this?"

"Because I've been following their whole operation, nigga, that's why."

"I feel you. What type of risk we talking?"

"It doesn't matter, nigga. Your bitch in jail, and you talking about risk. I don't know how much money it is, but anything helps when you need two million. Now, is you going to stay here looking like a bum, having a fucking pity party? Or, do you want to get this money?"

"Get this money, nigga," Sa'vere replied, giving Trell some dap.

"We making a move tonight, nigga. You need to take a shower and pull yourself together and get your head back in the damn game. Shit, they gonna *smell* you coming."

"Whatever, muthafucka."

"I'm gon' hit you with the time and place. I'm telling you, nigga, bring your fucking A-game. I know it's been awhile since you ran in a nigga's crib. You done got used to running in pussy instead."

"Nigga, trust me, some things are like riding a bike."

"A'ight, nigga, I'll hit your line."

"No doubt," Sa'vere said, giving his boy some dap before closing the door behind him. Trell was right. It had been a long time since he ran in a nigga's crib for that paper. That's all him and Trell did growing up. When he started finessing females out of money, they leaned off the hustle. He felt his inner savage coming alive by the second. He was a long way from two million but was ready to die to get it for his love. Hitting his blunt, he walked upstairs to get himself together.

***

Sa'vere had a long day thinking about whether Tay Tay would forgive him. All he knew was he was hungry for that bag and he was going to get it. He cocked his gun as Trell pulled his box Chevy around the corner.

"It's that blue house on the left. All we gotta do is pull around in the alley and hide on the far side of the house. As soon as that nigga comes out with that bag doing the drop for the night, we on his ass and in the back door. It's a camera over the door, so we gotta give them a chance to open it before we move. I don't know how many niggas in there, so be ready to lay a muthafucka down if you got to."

"Nigga, I ain't new to this."

"I'm just giving you a refresher course, nigga," Trell said, passing him the blunt.

"Whatever, nigga. Let's do this shit."

Trell looked at Sa'vere before putting the car in drive.

They had parked the car down the street in the alley behind an abandoned house before making their way toward the stash house. They were lucky the house next door was abandoned, so they used it to get on the far side of the house. They lay in the shadows for almost an hour before the car with the bag pulled up in front of the house.

"He coming, nigga!" Trell whispered as he ran back along the side of the house with his gun out. Sa'vere nodded, his black ski mask covering his face. It only took a few seconds for the heavyset, light-skinned man to get around the house with two black duffle bags. He set one down on the porch and knocked on the door. Sa'vere stood there like an Olympic runner, waiting on the starting pistol. When he saw the door open, he was out the gate like a greyhound at the derby.

The light-skinned dude had just grabbed the bag he set down when he heard footsteps approaching. He wanted to warn the others inside, but it was too late. Sa'vere mashed the barrel of his .45 automatic into his head, pushing him inside.

"Get on the fucking floor!" Sa'vere yelled, seeing three dudes in the house, but they weren't trying to hear what he was saying, especially the one who opened the door. He had raised his gun and pulled the trigger, but the bullet hit the man with the duffle bag instead. Sa'vere returned fire and his bullets hit his target in the upper neck and shoulder, dropping him to the floor. Trell didn't ask questions; he just came in shooting at the other two men grabbing guns off the money-covered kitchen table. Bullets flew everywhere, but the two men didn't stand a chance as Sa'vere and Trell sent shots in their direction. When the gunshots stopped, Sa'vere and Trell were the only ones standing with guns smoking as the two gunmen lay dead.

"Where's the rest of the money?" Trell asked the man who was carrying the bags as he tried to apply pressure to his stomach wound.

"It's in the fridge!" he whispered as a stream of blood ran out of his mouth. Sa'vere ran right to the fridge and opened it.

"Bingo!"

"Ted gone kill y'all."

"Nigga, fuck Ted and you!" Trell said, raising his gun and squeezing the trigger two times, putting bullets in the man's head. Sa'vere pulled a clear plastic bag out of his sleeve and started grabbing the neat bundles of cash that were stacked in the fridge from top to bottom instead of groceries.

It only took Sa'vere and Trell less than five minutes to fill up the bag and grab the other two duffle bags full of cash. They left nothing but the blood-scattered money on the table and four dead bodies behind.

"Nigga, hurry up and get it in!" Trell yelled, out of breath, as Sa'vere put his bag in the backseat.

"Let's go!" Sa'vere yelled, slamming his door, making Trell pull off.

"I told you, nigga, we done hit heavy," Trell said, taking his mask off as he pulled the car out of the alley.

"Hell, yeah, nigga!" Sa'vere said, lighting a Newport,

trying to calm his adrenaline down.

"You good, nigga?"

"Hell, yeah, is you good?" Sa'vere replied.

"Yeah, I'll be better when we count this money."

"No doubt," Sa'vere said, giving Trell some dap with his bloody glove.

***

The last few days had been long for Tay Tay and the fresh air on her face was much needed. Making the decision to sign the divorce papers and give him what he wanted was a gamble, but it was one she was willing to take. She needed her freedom, and her first stop was to her house to confront Wayne. It was almost 11:00 at night when Tay Tay's cab pulled up to their estate.

"Wait here," she said, passing him a one hundred-dollar bill out of the $10,000 Walter had given her upon release. He said the other $490,000 would be there in a couple of days. She wanted to kill him but knew Walter was just a pawn in Wayne's game. She approached the security gate and put her code in, but the screen said denied. She tried it three more times and the same thing happened. She then pushed the button to summon someone in the house.

"Wayne, quit fucking playing and open this damn gate!"

"Ummm, I'm sorry, but Wayne is busy," a voice said through the intercom catching Tay Tay off guard.

"Mesha?" Tay Tay said, confused.

"Yeah, it's me, bitch, and I would appreciate it if you would quit ringing my buzzer like that."

"Mesha, I'm going to kill you, bitch!"

"Is that a threat because I would sure hate to have these bond papers I got right here get revoked, considering my fiancé and I hold your bond. Now, if I were you, I'd get back in that cab you came in and ride out. This is *my* house now."

"Bitch, I swear to God—"

"You swear to God, what? Bitch, *I* deserve this life, *not* you. You and that bitch, Stacey, thought you were better than me. Both you hoes know I don't lose. Now, like I said, you need to get in that cab before your bond gets revoked, bitch. Thanks for visiting the Washington residence, ho, now *poof!* be gone." Tay Tay was so heated she couldn't even say anything else. She had been hurt worse than she ever had in her life over the last few days.

She got in the cab and slammed the door behind her.

"I need to go to Arlington Heights," Tay Tay said, passing the driver another hundred-dollar bill from her stash.

"No problem, ma'am," the black driver said, putting the car in drive.

"You got a cigarette by any chance?"

"Yeah, you can have the whole pack. Looks like you need them more than me," the driver replied, handing her his pack of Newport 100s and a lighter.

"Thanks," Tay Tay said, pulling one out and letting the window down before lighting it. The only thing that kept her from climbing that security gate and killing both of them was what her friend, Marisol, had told her before she got released. Tay Tay knew she had nothing to lose and everything to gain at this point, and there was no way in hell she was going to let them get away with playing her.

***

"Damn, nigga, that's $120,000. We should've taken the money counter too."

"This $80,000 here. I got a bunch of paper cuts, but fuck it. I know one thing, I need a fucking drink and some damn music to celebrate this wealth. It's too fucking quiet."

"Don't trip, nigga, I got that new Nick Flair; that shit's smackin'."

"I heard that. Yeah, put that shit on."

"I ain't got no Hennessey left, but I got some Rémy in the kitchen."

"That'll work, nigga." Sa'vere turned the surround sound on while Trell began breaking down a Backwoods before heading to the kitchen. Sa'vere opened the fridge door and moved a few things to get to the bottle.

"Here it goes right here," Sa'vere said thinking out loud. He stood up and closed the door . . . and the cold steel of a gun pressed firmly against his head.

"What the fuck?"

"Nigga, shut up!"

"Trell, quit playing!"

"Nigga, this ain't no fucking game. You made a living on playing a muthafucka, but you the one been getting played the whole time. Me and my baby, Mesha, played you like a sucka from the jump."

"Nigga, you tripping."

"Nah, nigga, *you* tripping. Thanks to you, we got inside

the biggest drug operations in the country, and you just helped me knock the competition out of the business. Now that we're done with you and that bitch, Tay Tay, I'm going to kill you and her just like I did her friend, Stacey. At the end of the day, it'll all look like a drug hit gone bad. Don't look stupid, nigga, like you was the only side nigga in the world. How's it feel to get played, nigga?"

"Fuck you!" Sa'vere said, closing his eyes, ready to take his last breath on earth.

"Nah, nigga, fuck *you*!" That was the last thing Sa'vere heard before the loud popping sound of a gun going off filled the room. Sa'vere didn't feel any pain, though; he had accepted that death was coming one day soon anyhow. Then he heard a loud thud that made him open his eyes.

Sa'vere could see the bullet hole in the back of Trell's dreads still smoking as blood poured out of the wound. He lay there twitching on the floor. Sa'vere looked up and saw Tay Tay standing there, holding his gun from off the table with the money they were counting. He still didn't know if he should move or not, but Tay Tay answered his question by lowering the gun and running into his arms.

"I swear, Taylor, I'm sorry for what I did. I love you so much, God only knows the depths."

"I love you too, Sa'vere. Please don't hurt me like that again. I know your words are true because I feel them in my soul," she said in his arms where she belonged. She was mad at Sa'vere, but hearing Trell's words verified that Sa'vere was just a pawn in the game like she had been. She didn't know if her heart was racing because she had killed a man for the first time in her life, or because she felt true love comforting her battered soul. Sa'vere slowly took the gun from her hand before speaking.

"Everything's going to be okay, boo, I promise, but right now, we need to clean this mess up. I need you to go to the store and get some bleach and duct tape. You gon' have to go buy it a ways away from here and make sure you pay in cash."

"Okay, Sa'vere," she said, trembling.

"Calm down, Taylor, I got this," Sa'vere said before kissing her on the forehead. He could see that she was a little shaken still, and he needed her to relax. He was probably the same way the first time he had killed someone, only he had no one to comfort him but the money. Looking her in the eyes, he leaned over, passionately kissing her soft lips.

"Okay, I got this, Sa'vere, trust me," she said, walking past the blood puddle and dead body on the floor. Even though she had never killed a man, she was happy she got the first-time jitters out of the way because Wayne and Mesha were on her hit list. She grabbed Sa'vere's car keys off the table.

Sa'vere stood there in the kitchen looking at his dead homie for a few minutes. He couldn't believe he was lying there dead. He could remember them talking about balling out together and shitting on all the haters. Now that was a thing of the past. Money and Mesha could make the snake come out of any nigga. Even though he felt bad, his heart was still cold, and his next words expressed it.

"Nah, nigga, it's fuck *you*!" he said, before pulling out his phone as he walked out of the kitchen.

"Big Meat, I need you like yesterday, nigga."

"What's going on?" Meat replied.

"I got some laundry that needs to go out before it gets to stinking."

"Oh shit, a'ight. Send me the address."

"Bet!" Sa'vere said before hanging up.

***

Tay Tay got everything she needed from the store, and when she returned, she saw a black truck parked in the driveway. She just grabbed the stuff and got out of the car, making her way into the house. She was surprised at what she saw when she walked in the door. Sa'vere was sitting on the couch with Big Meat smoking a blunt, laughing and joking. She looked at the floor and there was a carpet rolled up with what she assumed was Trell's body.

"Tay Tay, you remember my homie? This Meat. He 'bout to help us out," Sa'vere said as he got up and got the bag from Tay Tay while passing her the blunt.

"It's good to meet you again," Tay Tay said, hitting the blunt to calm her nerves.

"You too. This nigga like my little brother. His problems are my problems," he said, taking the duct tape from Sa'vere. Tay Tay didn't say anything, she just watched the two men go to work like they had done this before.

It took them about forty-five minutes to duct tape Trell's body in the rug, load him on the back of the truck, and clean up the murder scene.

"I would love to stay and play, but I got other things I gots to be doing," Big Meat said, giving Sa'vere a handshake and a half hug.

"No doubt, my nigga. I appreciate you," Sa'vere said, handing Meat $20,000.

"What's this extra $10,000 for?" Meat asked, reading the $10,000 money bands wrapped around the stacks he was holding.

"That's for you."

"You know you don't owe me nothing. You know we do this shit, nigga," Meat said, knowing Sa'vere had been there for him in situations worse than this.

"Fuck that, nigga, that's you."

"No doubt, bruh. Make sure you call that lawyer's number I gave you. She can get y'all right. When I get done handling this business outside in the truck, I'm going to drop this bread off to her, so she'll be expecting your call."

"Thanks, Big Meat," Tay Tay said, waving as the big man made his way out the door.

"I'm about to holler at Meat right fast. I'll be right back."

"Okay, I'm about to go run me a bath," Tay Tay said, blowing him a kiss before he walked out.

"Man, you know I really appreciate it, Meat."

"Nigga, don't worry about this shit. You need to go take care of that lady. I don't know what y'all plan on doing, but you know I'm down with whatever. You owe me so many security hours."

"I gotcha, I swear," Sa'vere said, giving him some more dap. Even though Meat ran the biggest security business in

Chicago, he also had his underworld lifestyle, which made him the man to make shit happen, especially for Sa'vere.

"I sure hate Trell gotta be put in the dirt, but, nigga, don't let that shit get you off your square. I know how close y'all was. Y'all was little niggas out here in these streets when I was just coming up. Sometimes your left hand gotta cut off your right hand before it poisons the body. You'd rather be missing your hand than be dead, I hope?"

"Hell, yeah, nigga. I feel you, though."

"Good, hit my line, bruh."

"Yep," Sa'vere said before heading back into the house. It had been a long day, and he wanted nothing else but to make sure Tay Tay was okay. He had almost lost her before, and he didn't plan on there being a second time, he thought to himself, closing the mansion door behind him.

***

Sa'vere had stayed up drinking and smoking, trying to get his mind right. It didn't matter how hard he partied the night before, he always woke up early. He usually beat Tay Tay up, but when he rolled over, no one was there. They didn't speak the night before after Tay Tay got out of the tub. After Sa'vere finished his drink, he just lay in the bed next to her, holding her close. He knew she had been through a lot, so he wasn't going to force any conversation. He had hurt her, and even though she forgave him, the wound still needed time to heal.

He got out of bed in his boxers, grabbed his blunt, and lit it before going to see where Tay Tay was. When he got to the stairs, he could see her sitting at the bottom of the staircase with a thin shirt on like she was thinking. He made his way down and sat behind her.

"You okay, boo?"

"Yeah. I just got a lot on my mind. I do forgive you, Sa'vere. I just need to know it's me and you against the world—no games."

"That's a promise. You all I need in this world. I want to take this money and just disappear to an island," he said, passing her the blunt.

"That would be nice, but fuck that. This money we got won't last us long. Wayne done broke me to get out of jail. Hopefully, this lawyer can do something for us. Wayne and Mesha moved in together."

"What?"

"Yeah, that bitch answered the intercom when I tried to confront him about playing me out of my money. Only thing good is I ain't married to that bum no more. We can build an empire way bigger than the one I built him."

"I'm with it, boo. Let's see what this lawyer is talking about, then we can go from there. I'm ten toes down for you," Sa'vere said, kissing her on the side of her neck.

She moaned slightly before hitting the blunt again. She then turned her head toward him and pressed her lips against his right before their tongues met in a cloud of weed smoke. Their love was long overdue, and within seconds, Tay Tay was on her back on the stairs, Sa'vere's tongue licking right down the middle of her soaking-wet pussy.

"Oh shit, nigga, damn. I missed you so much."

He responded by slurping all across that pussy before

licking it aggressively like he was trying to lick the soul out of her. She had been dreaming of him eating her pussy, and she was going to make sure he got every last drop of her come in his mouth. She grabbed the back of his head, grinding her pussy all over his face.

"Oh shit, I'm about to come all in your mouth, Sa'vere!" Her screams echoed through the mansion, her convulsions hard, making her legs almost lock around his head.

Sa'vere wasn't playing games with that pussy. He wiped his face before pulling his boxers down and pushing his dick all inside her tight, wet pussy. He took his time at first, long stroking that pussy as they both watched his dick going in and out of her.

"You my bitch?"

"Yes, Sa'vere, yes!" she pleaded as he began beating that pussy until you could hear a smacking sound with each stroke. Before she knew it, she was grabbing his arms with all her might as she screamed, coming back to back.

"Damn, you going to make me bust," Sa'vere said.

Tay Tay pulled his dick out of her pussy and sat up on the stairs, staring at his big, pretty come-dripping dick eye-to-eye like a snake charmer before taking him in her mouth.

"Shit, Tay Tay!" Sa'vere said as she deep throated his dick over and over until his load shot down her throat just like she liked it.

"Nigga, this dick is mine, and so are you, so don't you forget it," Tay Tay said, squeezing his dick, knowing it was sensitive.

"Okay, baby," Sa'vere said, happy his baby was his again.

"Let's get some breakfast and hit this lawyer up. We got an empire to start building."

"Well, let's do it then," Sa'vere said, slapping her across her phat, naked ass as she walked up the stairs.

"Go on, boy, you play too much," Tay Tay said, feeling like a piece of her shattered life was back in its proper position.

***

After getting dressed, Sa'vere and Tay Tay made their way to see the lawyer. Tay Tay had told Sa'vere how Wayne and Mesha were holding the bond over her head. Getting Tay Tay from under this case was Sa'vere's top priority.

"Welcome. Come on in and have a seat. I'm Ms. Conner, but y'all can call me Nicole," said the sharply dressed, young, mixed black woman. She wasn't what either of them expected to see, especially since she was sexy and thick, and both of them couldn't help but stare for a second.

"Well, my friend, Meat, tells me you got a problem. So, what I did was pull up all the information I could on you, Ms. Washington, soon-to-be Brown as filed by these divorce papers."

"That's correct. He blackmailed me into signing that and giving up all my rights to money, properties, and businesses just to get out of jail. Now, he's holding that over my head. He bought me the car that had the dope in it."

"I see. Do you know someone named J Mo?"

"Yes, that's my ex-husband's brother."

"Well, I did some digging, and this J Mo is a big man in the dope game, which I'm sure you already knew. But did you know that this man is also on his payroll?" Nicole asked, passing a photo across the table.

"You know him?" Sa'vere asked.

"Hell, yeah, that's the pig who arrested me," Tay Tay replied, seeing Detective Conan and J Mo talking in what looked like a surveillance photo.

"I have no doubt you've been set up. My surveillance team only started following him since last night, and he's dirty as they come. That picture was taken outside of J Mo's bar."

"So, what can we do about all this?" Sa'vere asked.

"Well, you guys can rest easy because getting cases beat is my thing. I usually charge $20,000 for a case like this, but I can't let you go out like that. The only thing we have a problem with is the stuff you agreed to. It's going to be hard to go back on that, but if they want to fight, we can fight."

"So, all my money just gone?"

"Not gone, just not in your possession right now. I know it isn't an easy pill to swallow, but this Wayne dude and his brother are some dirty muthafuckas. That's why I'm going to help y'all out."

"Thanks, we appreciate it!" Tay Tay said.

"Now, until your court date next week, I want y'all to lay low and stay out of trouble. Here's my card. Call me twenty-four seven. I work for y'all now," she said, getting up and shaking their hands. Tay Tay was pissed at the thought of being broke and played, but she felt confidence in the lawyer for some reason.

"We definitely about to lay low," Sa'vere said to Tay Tay with a look on his face like he'd take her down right there on the spot.

"Shut up, boy!" Tay Tay said, playfully hitting him.

"Ain't nothing wrong with a little laying low," Nicole said with a seductive smile.

Sa'vere and Tay Tay wanted to take Nicole down right with them. Tay Tay had never been with a female before, but if she did, she sure wouldn't mind Nicole feeding her that pussy. She could tell Nicole was reading their minds, but Tay Tay knew it was business before pleasure. She had built the drug empire that she had just lost on that motto, and she wasn't about to break it now.

"We'll definitely be in touch," Tay Tay said, pushing Sa'vere out the door.

"I'll be waiting," Nicole responded, giving them both a look like they could get it.

"Come on, boo. Soon as we get done with business, we gon' get that," Tay Tay said.

"See, you the real MVP."

"Shut up, nigga. We ain't gotta worry about cheating if we go get it together."

"I did tell you I love you, right?" Sa'vere said, smiling.

"Come on, boy, you play too much," she said as they walked out the lobby door.

Chapter 6

Shattered but Not Broken

The next week, Sa'vere and Tay Tay spent laid up in the mansion. It was like they had met each other all over again. Neither had anything to hide from each other any longer, and it made the love they had greater than either of them had ever felt in their lives. Tay Tay finally had the support she needed. She looked back at Sa'vere, her mother, and brother sitting patiently to see what was about to go on in court as her lawyer took her seat next to her. Tay Tay had to stop from looking at Nicole's thick thighs because she could feel herself getting wet thinking about her and Sa'vere fucking the shit out of her together.

"State vs Ms. Taylor Brown. Ms. Brown, how do you plead?"

"Not guilty," Tay Tay said, hoping she had said the right thing.

"Your Honor, may I approach?" Nicole asked, standing up.

"You may," the judge said. Nicole and the middle-aged,

white state's attorney approached the bench.

"I hope this is good, Counselor. I've got a full docket this morning," the grey-haired, black judge said, looking at Nicole.

"Your Honor, I hate to be wasting the court's time, though I can't say the same for the state. I have here frame-by-frame photos from the diner where my client was arrested. Here's the report from a Detective Conan that says she was pulled over for speeding. These photos clearly show differently," Nicole said, handing the judge time-stamped photos showing Tay Tay from the time she went into the restaurant until the time she was arrested.

"Your Honor, I object to these photos. I knew nothing about them," the state's attorney said, looking nervous. He had heard of Nicole Conner just like the rest of the legal system. He knew that she was one of the best attorneys around. Her looks were just as deadly as her tactics, and he was getting a taste of it firsthand.

"Well, this is pretty serious. Regardless of what was found, when officers lie like this, it leaves room for argument as to how they knew the perpetrators were there and if they planted the evidence themselves. I suggest you do a formal investigation into this. I'm sorry, but I'm going to have to dismiss this case. Ms. Brown, the bond is dropped, and your passport will be reinstated."

"How about her car, Your Honor?" Nicole asked, walking back toward Tay Tay. The judge couldn't help but look at her and just shake his head.

"She gets her car back as well. Everything except the drugs, how about that?" the judge said, slamming his gavel down. The state's attorney couldn't believe what just happened, and neither could Tay Tay.

"I told you, I got y'all," Nicole said to Tay Tay when she returned to her seat.

"Thank you so much," Tay Tay said, standing up and hugging her. Tay Tay ran toward her people, and they all headed out of the courtroom.

"We celebrating tonight."

"You damn right, we are," Tay Tay said, kissing Sa'vere as he hugged her.

"We might as well stop and get some E&J on the way home, Snoop."

"There you go, Mama, damn."

"Boy, shut up and let's go. All these police make my ass itch."

"We'll see y'all at the house, sis," Snoop said, hugging his sister.

"Okay, we're about to go see how to get my car back, and we'll be there."

"A'ight," Snoop replied, following his mother. Sa'vere and Tay Tay waited on Nicole who wasn't far behind.

"Well, I think your car is in the impound. Here are the court papers."

"Thanks."

"Is there anything else you need?" Nicole asked.

"Well, we're having a private celebration tonight for this victory. You might want to come through and join us," Tay Tay suggested.

"Sounds interesting. I think I just might have to come through. Are there going to be a lot of people?"

"Three when you get there," Sa'vere added.

"Well, in that case, send me the address."

"I sure will," Tay Tay said.

"Y'all enjoy your day. Don't forget to send that address," Nicole reminded them before turning to walk away. Sa'vere and Tay Tay just stared for a second.

"Send the address, Tay Tay, quit playing."

"I ain't playing, trust that," she replied, pulling her phone out to text the address.

***

After getting Tay Tay's Bentley coupe back, they spent the rest of the day at Tay Tay's mother's house partying. When Tay Tay got the text around ten from Nicole asking if the party was still on, they knew it was time for the after-party at the mansion, and Sa'vere and Tay Tay made sure they were ready for it. Ecstasy filled their bodies and Hennessey was their chaser as they heard the doorbell ring. Tay Tay had on a blue catsuit that matched her hair and hugged her thick body like a glove. Sa'vere had been doing his best to maintain his composure watching Tay Tay and all that ass as she walked. Tay Tay looked back at him to make sure he was watching and blew him a kiss with her juicy lips. She then turned back around and opened the door.

"Hey, Nicole, how are you doing? Did you find the place okay?"

"Yeah, my GPS brought me right here," Nicole replied. Sa'vere was like a kid at the candy store as he looked at Tay Tay and Nicole who had on a black dress so tight it looked like you would have to peel it off.

"That's good. I still be getting lost," Tay Tay said, making them laugh as she closed the door behind Nicole. Tay Tay couldn't help but look down at Nicole's ass, and then back up at Sa'vere and wink, giving her seal of approval for Nicole without her knowing.

"Well, I see y'all started the celebration without me," Nicole said, walking toward the huge couch Sa'vere was sitting on. A fifth of Hennessey Paradise sat on the table next to two half-empty glasses.

"Trust, we got plenty."

"That's good, I like plenty," Nicole said, giggling seductively.

"Well, we might as well get this party started. Come on, let's go out back," Tay Tay said, leading the way. Sa'vere grabbed the bottle and took a big gulp as he followed both women.

"Thank you, Jesus," he whispered to himself, seeing all that ass in front of him.

"Wow, this is really nice!" Nicole said upon seeing the massive screened-in patio with an endless swimming pool. The couches were just as big as the ones inside the house. The fire pit was burning perfectly.

"I'm happy you like it. Come on, let's get that drink," Tay Tay said. They walked toward a door on the back side of the house and went into a room that looked like the perfect man cave. A white leather pool table that matched the white leather furniture was in the middle of the floor. A top-of-the-line bar sat fully stocked near an eighty-inch plasma TV that almost covered a wall.

"Well, I guess I spoke too soon. This place is fucking bad as hell. Must've cost a fortune."

"It used to be some celebrity's home. I found a solid line on closed properties that lets me get first dibs right as the paperwork hits the bank's desk. The bank would rather sell the properties dirt cheap than do all the work of putting it on the market."

"That's quite the hustle. You need to let me know what I have to do to get me a house like this. I got a couple of dollars put up."

"I gotcha, girl."

Sa'vere went behind the bar like a bartender. "What can I get you ladies to drink?"

"Well, what do you suggest?" Tay Tay said. "Maybe the Goose, maybe this Don Julio."

"What do you think, Nicole?"

"Shit, might as well have one of each. It's Friday, and I done cut my phone off till Monday," Nicole replied, making them all laugh as she sat on the white leather bar stool next to Tay Tay.

The next couple of hours, they drank and laughed while enjoying the TV and the Drake Pandora station playing over the surround sound. Sa'vere was sitting on the bar smoking a Backwoods as the females danced by the pool table.

"I ain't never played pool before. Somebody gotta teach me. I always wanted to play," Nicole said, grabbing the pool stick that was on the table.

"Tay Tay, you might as well teach her; you're better than me."

"Whatever, nigga."

"Come on, Tay Tay," Nicole said, walking to the top of the table. She acted like she was trying to hit the ball with the pool stick, but she couldn't even hold it the right way, and it ended up slipping out of her grip.

"See, Tay Tay, I really need some help."

"I feel the same way," Tay Tay said as she walked toward Nicole.

"So, at least tell me, am I holding the stick right?" Nicole said, bent over the table like she was about to take another shot.

"Yeah, let me help you," Tay Tay said, walking up behind her. Tay Tay pressed her already throbbing pussy against Nicole's phat ass like she was about to help her shoot. Tay Tay couldn't help but grind against Nicole who threw her ass right back against her and gave out a slight moan. Nicole turned around until they were face-to-face. The ladies' lips and tongues met aggressively like they had been waiting for each other all night long. Their kisses continued as Tay Tay helped Nicole up on the pool table as she pulled her tight dress up and around her phat ass. Tay Tay's lips continued down Nicole's neck until she pulled Nicole's titties out and put one in her mouth before sucking hard on her erect nipples. Her mouth found the other nipple and sucked it before flicking her tongue against it.

"Oh yeah, I like that," Nicole said, spreading her legs as Tay Tay began looking down at her phat pussy that was leaking all over her red lace panties. Nicole put her hand in her panties and rubbed all over her pussy. She then pulled her hand out and held it up so Tay Tay could taste her juices off her fingers.

Tay Tay moaned softly as she enjoyed every drop, making her want more. She began at Nicole's inner left knee and kissed and sucked up Nicole's thigh until she could see the lips of her pussy peeking out from the side of her panties. She had always wanted to try this, and now, here she was, she thought to herself.

Nicole pulled her panties to the side and grabbed the back of Tay Tay's head, pulling her face into her leaking, wet pussy. Tay Tay loved the way she tasted, and the effects from the Ecstasy made Tay Tay lick all in that pussy like a savage.

"Oh my God. Oh my God, oh my God!" Nicole yelled out in pleasure as she grinded her pussy all over Tay Tay's face and tongue until her thighs began trembling.

"Oooh, I'm going to come all in your mouth!"

And Tay Tay wanted her to. Nicole's words only made her slurp and lick harder until come squirted into her mouth. Tay Tay tried to drown in that pussy as she kept licking, forcing Nicole to beg her to stop as she kept coming and convulsing. Tay Tay stood up while Nicole tried to recover on the table. She looked at Sa'vere as she began peeling off her catsuit.

"Come on, baby, come get you some of this good-ass pussy. We 'bout to make you our bitch," Tay Tay said.

"Yes, make me y'all's bitch!" Nicole replied, squeezing her titties together with both hands as she spread her legs wide.

Sa'vere hit the bottle of Hennessey and wiped his mouth before jumping off the bar. He had enjoyed the show, and his dick was hard as a rock. He walked over to Tay Tay and kissed her on her mouth, tasting Nicole's juices on her lips. She pulled the condom out of his jeans pocket before pulling his zipper down; his rock-hard dick sprang out, ready to play. She helped it by pulling his boxers and pants down. She ripped the gold magnum condom wrapper open with her teeth and pulled the condom out. Then she bent over and took that dick slowly in her mouth as Nicole watched while playing with her leaking pussy. Tay Tay pulled Sa'vere's dick out of the back of her throat and rolled the condom on his throbbing dick.

"Make that bitch ours!" Tay Tay whispered to him, stroking his dick one last time. Sa'vere didn't have to be told twice; he pulled his wife beater over his head and threw it to the floor like it was time to go to work. He turned around to Nicole and walked right up to the table and snatched her to the edge of the pool table. He cuffed her thighs over his biceps and lifted her bottom half up in the air as his dick spread her pussy out inch by inch until he felt his balls smack her ass. He stirred in that pussy and grinned as her eyes rolled back in her head.

"Oh my God!" Nicole screamed out as Sa'vere started beating that pussy crazy. Before Nicole could scream again, Tay Tay had straddled her face. Tay Tay fucked Nicole's face while Sa'vere continued to hold that pussy up in the air as he tried to knock the back out of that pussy. She tried to scream but Tay Tay's pussy gave her a mouth full.

"Yeah, I told you that we were gonna make you ours, bitch," Tay Tay said before coming in Nicole's mouth. Between Sa'vere fucking the shit out of her and the taste of

Tay Tay's come running out of her pussy and into her mouth, Nicole found herself coming hard all over Sa'vere's dick. Tay Tay climbed off Nicole's face while Sa'vere continued his assault on her pussy.

"Beat our pussy up! You our bitch, ain't you?"

"Yes yes yes!"

"Tell me you our bitch!"

"I'm y'all's bitch, I'm y'all's bitch, I swear."

Sa'vere fucked her as hard and as fast as he could until he bust his load all in the condom.

"Goddamn," Nicole said, unable to do anything but lay back on the pool table and close her eyes as Sa'vere put her down. Two minutes later, Nicole was out for the count in the same position she lay down in. Tay Tay just smiled with a devilish grin on her face. Making her man fuck the shit out of a bad bitch like Nicole wasn't in a basic female's interest. She felt a little bad using Sa'vere to hook Nicole just like she had been hooked, but she knew they was going to need a powerful lawyer because if Wayne and Mesha thought she was bowing out of the game, they had another think coming.

"I love you!" she said to Sa'vere.

"I love you too," he replied, not knowing that he had just been enlisted in Tay Tay's army.

***

It was almost five in the morning when Nicole came walking out of the man cave wrapped in the blanket that Tay Tay had covered her up in while she slept on the pool table.

"Damn, you're up early," Tay Tay said, sitting on the outdoor sectional couch wrapped in her blanket in front of the fire pit, smoking a blunt. The effects of the Ecstasy wouldn't let her sleep.

"Shit, I don't even remember going to sleep."

"Yeah, it was a long night. I hope you enjoyed yourself."

"Hell, yeah, I enjoyed myself," Nicole said, sitting down on the couch.

"Good, we did too. We were talking about it until he passed out on me," Tay Tay said, laughing.

"A place like this and the people out to get you lets me know you're into something far bigger than real estate. That divorce was crazy. Wayne and his brother were definitely behind you going to jail. How much of the business do you know?"

Tay Tay looked like she wanted to answer but didn't.

"It's okay, we have attorney-client privilege."

"I know the whole operation. I built it."

"Well, I don't know if Big Meat told you or not, but outside of being one of the baddest attorneys around, I also provide a service for my *special* clients."

"I'm listening."

"I have some individuals looking for a strong connect. If I can provide that, I make a finder's fee. Y'all can do your business, and I'll be your attorney if something happens."

"That's some good stuff to know. I just might take you up on it."

"Like I told you, if there's anything you need, I gotcha."

"Well, since you saying that, I need you to get over here

and eat this pussy," Tay Tay said, opening her blanket, exposing her naked body. She lay back on the couch, still smoking her blunt. Nicole didn't hesitate to follow Tay Tay's directions and went face-first into Tay Tay's pussy as she spread her thighs.

"Yeah, eat that pussy till I come all in your mouth," Tay Tay said, grabbing the back of Nicole's head while still smoking her blunt. Tay Tay slow grinded her pussy all around Nicole's face and tongue.

"Ooh, you taste so good," Nicole said before slurping on that pussy like a melting Popsicle in the summertime.

"Yes, eat that pussy, bitch; you 'bout to make me come," Tay Tay said as she felt herself reaching her climax, leaking come into Nicole's eager mouth.

"Yeah, feed me all that come!"

Tay Tay held on to the back of Nicole's head, making sure she got every last drop.

"Yeah, you our bitch now!" Tay Tay said, rubbing Nicole's head as she just lay down on her in between her legs.

"Yes, I am," Nicole said followed by a slight moan.

Tay Tay knew that by the end of the weekend with Sa'vere fucking her brains out and her feeding her pussy, Nicole was definitely going to be theirs.

***

After a long weekend of taking advantage of Nicole, Tay Tay was ready for straight business when Monday came around. She and Sa'vere were at her mother's house early. Ms. Brown cooked breakfast, and they ate good. As soon as breakfast was over, Tay Tay, Sa'vere, and Snoop made their way out back.

"What's going on with y'all?"

"Shit, bruh, I needed to sit down and holler at you about something." When they sat down, she continued. "I know I told you about Wayne and Mesha, but I got a plan."

"Yeah, 'cause that nigga's ass is mine," Snoop said. He had been pissed since Tay Tay told him about how he and Mesha set her up.

"We're going to have plenty of time for that. Right now, we need to focus on this money. I built that empire, and I'll build another bigger and better than that one. All I need is to make sure you're on board 'cause shit can get real."

"Sis, you know I'm born ready." Snoop couldn't help but smile, hearing the inner drug lord come out of his sister.

"Well, the three of us are all we got to make this happen. I'm trying to let things cool off with these police on my ass thanks to these muthafuckas. My main problem right now is where we're going to move the product if I make this move to get it."

"Shit, I got the hotel still. I know you didn't approve of me staying there, but like I told you, it's plenty money," Sa'vere said, lighting the Backwoods he had rolled.

"I got these streets on lock. All I need is the demo, and it's on."

"Let's get to this money, then. I'm waiting on a few things to put it in order, but we gonna make this shit happen," Tay Tay said when the back screen door opened and Alisha popped out.

"Is Mama out here?"

"Nope, she gone with Auntie somewhere," Snoop said.

"Tell her I came by to let Jabari see her," Alisha said, going back in the house.

"I'll be right back," Tay Tay said, getting up from the backyard card table.

"You cool, sis?"

"Yeah, I'm cool, nigga, damn," Tay Tay said, walking toward the house.

Alisha was in the fridge when she came in and Jabari was in a trance in front of the TV watching SpongeBob.

"Alisha, I'm sorry. I know I should've did more, but I was young and dumb and got so caught up with this man, I couldn't break free. There ain't no excuse for what I did. You're my sister, and I love you to death, girl."

"I love you too, Tay Tay," Alisha replied, giving her sister a much-needed hug.

"We have to go somewhere, do some shopping and catch up."

"Well, only on one condition."

"What's that?"

"I get to drive the Bentley."

"A'ight. You got a deal," Tay Tay said, smiling.

"Jabari, get your coat, boy. Auntie Tay Tay 'bout to take us shopping in style."

Tay Tay loved the feeling of her whole family being happy, and she planned on keeping it that way. She hated that she had to start over, but she had a stronger foundation this time, and she'd be damned if they fell again.

***

The minishopping spree was just what Tay Tay and her sister needed. They caught up on each other's lives. Tay Tay told her about Wayne and Mesha, and Alisha told her all about her trifling baby daddy that was in jail and had her raising Jabari alone.

"Stop at the store so we can get some drinks and shit. I know Mama probably need some E&J and Squares. You want something?"

"Yeah, get me some Squares too. Mama be acting funny with hers."

"What you drink?"

"Whatever y'all drinking."

"Okay, I'll be right back."

Tay Tay was in the store for about five minutes before she came back out with a big bag in her hand.

"Dang, you got a big ole bag."

"I bought a gallon of Hennessey. I figured I missed your twenty-first birthday. We gotta make up for it."

"Well, turn up, then," Alisha said, pulling off.

"Here, Jabari, look what Auntie got you," Tay Tay said, passing him a Spider-Man ice-cream bar that made his eyes light up.

"What you say?" Alisha said to Jabari.

"Thank you, Auntie Tay Tay."

"You're welcome," Tay Tay said, turning back around as they pulled up at the red light.

"I can't believe I'm driving a Bentley. My friends gon' envy me."

"Soon as I get right, I'm gonna get you one, watch."

"Hell, yeah, sis. *That's* what I'm talking about," Alisha

said, turning her head and looking at the black Chevy Caprice that pulled up next to them fast.

"Pull off!" Tay Tay yelled, but by the time Alisha heard her, gunfire erupted from the passenger window of the Chevy Caprice. A masked man with a hood shot through the car with a handgun. The thirty-plus bullets from the extended clip came fast, but to Tay Tay, everything seemed to be going on slow motion. She had her eyes closed from the bullets shattering the window, and all she heard was the screeching tires of the Chevy pulling off.

"Alisha!" Tay Tay screamed, seeing her bloody and slumped over. She didn't know if she was hit or not, but she quickly put her leg over Alisha, hitting the brake, to stop the car from rolling. Tay Tay put the car in PARK and could see a lot of blood on Alisha's left side. Tay Tay looked in the backseat and her heart almost dropped. Jabari had ice cream all over his mouth that she had bought him . . . with a bullet hole in his forehead.

"Somebody help me, please!" Tay Tay screamed in a panic. She tried to calm down as she felt herself hyperventilating. She wondered if she was hit too, but that was the last thought she had as she felt light-headed and passed out.

***

The emergency room waiting area was packed but Snoop, Sa'vere, Ms. Brown, her sister, Stella, and Tay Tay weren't going anywhere. Tay Tay hadn't been hit by a bullet but had passed out from shock. Everyone's heart was broken into a million pieces since Jabari was pronounced dead on the scene. They had been crying for hours and wondering if Alisha was going to pull through.

"Ms. Brown?"

"Yes," Tay Tay's mother said, standing up along with everyone else.

"I'm Dr. Strauss. I'm sorry about your loss earlier. Your daughter suffered five bullet wounds. The worst one punctured a lung. She also lost a large amount of blood. She made it through surgery and is in critical condition. Right now, she's in a coma," said the black, middle-aged clean-cut doctor.

"Oh my God. Please don't take my baby!" Ms. Brown said almost passing out. She would've been on the floor if Snoop and Sa'vere hadn't caught her.

"Somebody get my mom some water, please!" Tay Tay yelled as Sa'vere and Snoop sat her down on a chair. The nurses quickly came to assist them.

"This is my fault!" Tay Tay said crying before she stormed off.

"Go get her, bruh, I got Mama," Snoop said.

"I got her," Sa'vere answered before walking off.

When Sa'vere caught up with her, she was sitting in the hallway on the floor crying. "Tay Tay, baby, come here," Sa'vere said as he helped her up off the floor.

She broke down crying in his arms. He felt a tear running down his face as he held her tight, feeling her pain in his soul.

"Everything's going to be all right."

"It hurts so bad, Sa'vere."

"I know, baby," he said, kissing her on her forehead. He

wished he could bear the pain of her shattered heart, but he knew nothing but time healed these kinds of wounds, so all he could do was comfort her.

"Excuse me, I hate to interrupt, but we're looking to talk to Ms. Taylor Brown. I'm Detective Matthews, and this my partner, Detective Craig," said the middle-aged white detective as he introduced himself and his black partner.

"That's me."

"We're sorry about your loss, but we need to talk to you down at the station."

"For what?" Sa'vere asked, getting heated.

"This is routine when there is a homicide," Detective Craig said, getting in the conversation.

"Calm down, baby, it's okay. Call our lawyer and meet me at the station. Please make sure Mama is okay."

"I will, boo," Sa'vere said, kissing her on the lips before she followed the police down the hall.

"Where's Tay Tay?" Snoop asked when he returned.

"She had to go down to the station for questioning. I'm about to call our lawyer and meet her down there. Where's your mom at?"

"They took her back. Here comes the doctor now."

"We're putting your mom on an IV and giving her something to calm her down. She has had a lot on her in a short time."

"I appreciate it, Doc. Between me and you, what are my sister's chances?"

"To be honest, they are slim, but she's a fighter."

"I feel you, Doctor."

"Excuse me, gentlemen, I have to get this call," the

doctor said, looking at his phone as he walked away before answering it.

"Wayne, I was just about to call you. They hit the wrong target."

"You gotta be fucking kidding me!"

"Nope, the baby died, and the sister is on life support. Your ex-wife walked away without a scratch."

"Fuck, these idiots can't do shit right."

"Well, I gotta go. Are we gonna get that shipment in soon? I have my people on hold, but they're not gonna wait forever when there's plenty other dealers lurking."

"Trust me, I got you. It's going to be worth the wait. Keep an eye on things and let me know if anything changes."

"No problem," the doctor said, hanging up the phone before heading back to the ICU.

***

"So, you're telling me you didn't see the people that shot in your car?" Detective Matthews asked as he paced the interrogation room floor.

"It all happened so fast."

"Too fast? Come on. I'll tell you what I think. I think this was a hit after the drugs you had got lost when you were arrested, and I know you know exactly who's responsible." Tay Tay was ready to lash out but a knock on the door interrupted them.

"This interview is over. My client has had enough pressure for one night. If you have any more questions, you can contact my office and we'll be happy to inform our client. Any other forms of contact will be considered harassment, and trust me, gentlemen, I will file a lawsuit without a second thought," Nicole said. Tay Tay just smiled as she stood up from her seat.

"Have a nice day, Officers," Tay Tay said, waving as she followed her lawyer out.

"I know that bitch knows something or has something to do with this. She can laugh now, but I promise, she's gonna fuck up, and we'll be right there with the cuffs for her ass," Detective Matthews said, pissed.

"You damn right!" Detective Craig said, giving his partner some dap. They were the Major Crimes Unit that dealt with high-level drug dealers. It was rare that they missed their target. Tay Tay was now on their radar.

**

Tay Tay had a long day and night. She now rode in the passenger seat of Nicole's Audi A8. Snoop had said he wanted Tay Tay to get some rest and he'd call her if anything changed at the hospital. The first part of the ride was quiet for her, Sa'vere, and Nicole. Then Nicole broke the silence.

"I would've been at the hospital had I known what happened."

"It's all good, I know you would have. All of this is like one big nightmare," Tay Tay said.

"What's this shit up ahead?" Nicole asked, seeing a police officer blocking the street headed to Tay Tay and Sa'vere's mansion.

"Sorry, this road is blocked off. There's a fire at the

mansion."

"That's my home!"

Tay Tay, and Sa'vere got out of the car. They had been so deep in thought, they hadn't noticed the sounds of the sirens or the cloud of smoke filling the late-night air.

"Let them through. They are the home owners," the police officer said to another cop.

"Come this way," the other officer said, walking them up the street around the corner where the house was visible.

"You gotta be fucking kidding me," Sa'vere said, seeing the massive house going up in flames as firefighters tried to put the fire out.

"I hope y'all had insurance. I don't think there's going to be a lot to save," the officer said before walking away.

"All our money was in the house," Tay Tay said as she and Sa'vere watched everything they had left in this world burn.

"Muthafuckas gotta pay!"

"You muthafuckin' right!" Tay Tay said, holding his hand and leaning her head on his shoulder.

***

Nicole had let them stay at her condo and was gone by the time Tay Tay and Sa'vere woke up. She had left a set of keys, $10,000, and a note that read:

I'll see y'all later. That's all the money I had on me, but I hope it helps with something. That's a house key and a key to the car in the garage. Love, Nicole.

"*That's* what's up. It wasn't the quarter million we had, but it's something," Sa'vere said, thumbing through the money. Tay Tay was about to respond, but her phone started ringing. She took a deep breath, hoping it wasn't a phone call saying her sister didn't make it. The number was blocked, and Tay Tay never answered blocked numbers, but with all that was going on, she had no choice.

"Hello."

"Hey, bestie, I was just calling to check on you and your broke-ass life. I hope you ain't holding no hard feelings toward me. I really miss you, Tay Tay."

"Mesha, I swear I'm going to kill you, bitch."

"I'm not worried about it. You see what condition your sister, your nephew, and your home ended up in. See, I was just calling to be nice, but you done made me mad now. Well, have a blessed day. Me and Wayne are running late for our honeymoon in the Bahamas. Oh, there's Mr. Washington calling his new Mrs. Washington now. Gotta go. Smooches," Mesha said before hanging up.

"I swear to God, both of them gotta suffer if it's the last thing I do on this earth!" Tay Tay said, pissed.

"Only way we gon' make them suffer is to hurt that money."

"You right, baby," Tay Tay said like a lightbulb had gone off in her head. She scrolled through her call log and found a number and clicked on it to send a text.

It's Tay Tay. Can I see you?

Tay Tay waited a few seconds in silence while Sa'vere wondered what she was doing. Then a notification sounded and she read a text that said, **1329 Glenn Street. Come alone.**

Give me an hour or so, she texted back.

K, was the response.

"I gotta handle something alone."

"Alone? Are you crazy? People are trying to kill you!"

"I know, baby, but you gotta trust me. Ain't nobody gonna have me hiding in no house."

"Well, at least let me get you a gun first," Sa'vere said, seeing by the look in Tay Tay's eyes that she was determined and wasn't going to take no for an answer.

"Okay, let me get my purse," Tay Tay said, wondering why that address sounded so familiar. She had never carried a gun before, but she thought it was about time she started.

It didn't take Sa'vere long to get Tay Tay a gun. One phone call to Meat was all it took. Through all the years she had been in the dope game, she'd never been paranoid like this. While riding to her destination, she was looking in the rearview with her gun on her lap. When Tay Tay pulled up to the gate at the address, she put her gun in her purse, especially since she saw security approaching with guns on their hips. She let down the window of the black BMW 750 Nicole had let her use.

"I'm here to see Marisol. My name is Tay Tay," she said, looking like she might be at the wrong address.

"One second," the big white security guard said before talking into his walkie-talkie. Tay Tay sat patiently for a few minutes before he returned.

"Go ahead," the guard said waving her into the opening gate. The mansion she pulled in front of was twice the size of one she'd just lost. Armed security was everywhere. Tay Tay didn't get any relief until she saw Marisol come out of the front door waving and smiling from ear to ear. Tay Tay left her purse in the car and made her way to Marisol.

"Heeeey, mami!" Marisol said, hugging Tay Tay like a long lost sister.

"Hey, girl, look at you. I was worried you wasn't out yet," Tay Tay replied, looking at how sexy Marisol looked outside of that County Jail uniform.

"What's wrong, Tay Tay? Is it Wayne's punta ass?" Marisol said, hating Wayne based on the stories Tay Tay had told her while they were cell mates.

"Girl, it's a long story."

"Well, come on in, chica. We got some catching up to do," Marisol said, putting her arm around Tay Tay's shoulders as she walked her into the megamansion.

The next hour, Tay Tay told Marisol what had happened to her from Mesha crossing her to her house burning down with all of her money inside, while they smoked high-grade weed. Tay Tay had needed to vent and get some air and didn't even mind when Marisol had left her outside for twenty minutes by herself.

"Tay Tay, come on, chica. There's someone I want you to meet," Marisol said, popping her head out of the glass sliding door. Tay Tay got up from her sun chair and followed Marisol.

"I'm sorry I took so long but your story is crazy. I think I got somebody that could help you."

"Okay. I'll take any help I can get right now," Tay Tay said, following Marisol upstairs and to a big door. Marisol opened the door.

"Mama, it's me and my chica."

"Come on in," a well-dressed, beautiful Latino woman said, getting up from her expensive desk. Tay Tay didn't even get to say anything before the lady was hugging her.

"It's nice to meet you."

"Oh, sweetie, you've been through a lot. My daughter told me everything. Some of these men need their balls cut off and fed to them," the woman said.

"Mama!" Marisol said, embarrassed.

"Girl, it's okay, she's telling the truth."

"Mama, this is Tay Tay. Tay Tay, this is my mom, Juanita Calderon."

"Juanita Calderon? But your name is Salazar."

"Yeah, that's her good-for-nothing father's last name, God rest his soul," Ms. Calderon said, walking back to her seat. Tay Tay was almost shook, like she had met a celebrity. In the dope game, Juanita Calderon was the Jay Z of dope dealers.

"Y-y-you're like the biggest drug dealer in the Southern Hemisphere," Tay Tay said, starstruck.

"They say that. I'd say the world," the Mexican woman said, making them all laugh before continuing. "So, my daughter tells me you need cocaine and a lot of it." The devilish grin on Tay Tay's face was all the answer Juanita needed, especially since hers matched.

"Surviving this game over the years has taken a lot of work. With all the snitches and government agencies, it's hard for me to even be in the country anymore. Only reason I'm here now is because my daughter just got out of jail.

Running business from afar was easier when Marisol's older brothers were alive, but now I'm forced to trust a bunch of yes-men that followed them. I want to put this business in the hands of my daughter, but I know she can't do it alone. Tay Tay, do you believe in fate?"

"Yes, ma'am," Tay Tay said, smiling, thinking about Sa'vere.

"Good, because I do believe we all are here together for a reason today. Running the old operation is a thing of the past. What I need is a new operation outside of these snakes my sons left behind. They are constantly defying the Calderon name. They even had my Marisol set up. I thought about killing them all, but there's no point when we can pay them back by eliminating their product. The only thing about that is we have to double the numbers they are doing. Times have changed, and the Calderon operation has to do the same. This new operation has multiple products. I'm talking A-1 cocaine, the highest quality heroin, guns, and an endless supply of pharmaceuticals. All we need is a place to put them, and from what my daughter has told me about you, I think you might have the answer." Juanita Calderon's words had Tay Tay's mind going a hundred miles an hour just like when she started helping Wayne and J Mo build the empire they snatched from under her.

"We can handle that, Ms. Calderon. I have a network for everything on the table," Tay Tay said, knowing she was lying.

"That's good to hear. A week from now, we will begin our new operation. Taylor, Marisol is all I had in this world until today. I accept you like a daughter, and I promise you that will come with a heavy price for anyone that crosses our family."

"Welcome to the family, sis," Marisol said, giving Tay Tay a hug.

"Thank you, Marisol, I swear. Thank you, Ms. Calderon, I'm so grateful for y'all," Tay Tay said, giving Ms. Calderon a hug next, whose arms received her like she would her own daughter.

"Come on, sis, we gotta plan a celebration," Marisol said, taking Tay Tay by the hand, excited that her mother accepted Tay Tay. This was not only a second chance for Tay Tay but a second chance for herself as well.

Ms. Calderon couldn't do anything but smile as Marisol and Tay Tay exited her office like they had won a Super Bowl. She hadn't smiled in a while, and she was definitely smiling now. When her daughter had told her about a female in jail that had got caught with major weight and had been set up by her husband, she had thought her daughter was just talking. Now that she had met her former cellie in the flesh, she could see the same pain in her eyes from an abusive husband that she'd seen in her own eyes for many years. That is, before she killed her husband, Marisol's father, and took his position on top of the dope game. Even though it had been twenty years ago, she still remembered it like it was yesterday.

Coming from one of the richest drug families in the world, they threw lavish parties all the time, and tonight was no different. Juanita Calderon's father and all the guests had just left, so there was no one left but her two sons and daughter, who were fast asleep, and their father and her husband, Ra'mon. She had met Ra'mon on a trip to the United States. He was not only the best lover she had ever met, but also the plug that put the Calderon drug operation ahead of everyone else supplying the United States. Juanita was the only child, and her father had loved Ra'mon like the son he never had. In his eyes, Ra'mon could do no wrong. He was perfect in many people's eyes, and his charisma kept them thinking that way. Unfortunately for Juanita, she knew the real animal that hid beneath his handsome smile, and the liquor and cocaine always seemed to summon him out of hiding.

"Juanita, where the fuck is the rest of the powder at? You always touching my shit!" the Spanish man said, still in his white suit.

"I haven't seen it, Ra'mon," Juanita said as she brushed her long hair in the mirror, getting ready for bed.

"You stupid lying whore, I know you got my shit!" he said, storming out of the room. Juanita knew he had way too much cocaine and alcohol, so she hid the cocaine he was using like she normally did when he had had too much. She knew eventually he would give up looking for it and pass out. All she had to do was not provoke him until he did. She continued enjoying the next five minutes of silence and had hoped he had fallen asleep but her hope was shattered by the fast-approaching footsteps of Ra'mon. Juanita looked toward him and could see he looked like a man possessed with a knife in his hand.

"Ra'mon!" Juanita yelled at him, trying to snap him out of the demented trance he was in, but her words fell on deaf

ears. She wanted to move, but her legs didn't get the memo, and Ra'mon's closed fist came crashing against her jaw, knocking her to the floor.

"You fucking bitch, you think you gonna keep hiding my shit like I'm fucking stupid? I'm the reason for all this, and you need to be reminded."

Juanita tried to get up after hearing his words, but the blow had her woozy and left her at his mercy. The next thing she knew, she was being dragged by the same hair she had just been brushing. Juanita kicked and tried to shake loose as he dragged her into the bathroom.

"Please, Ra'mon, stop, papi!" Ra'mon's only response was stomping her in the stomach with all his might. The pain was excruciating, and Juanita balled up instantly in the fetal position, trying to breathe. She could hear Ra'mon opening a bathroom cabinet, but she didn't know what he what was doing. By the time she looked up, she could see Ra'mon standing over her with the knife in one hand and a kilo of cocaine in the other. He smiled before he ran the razor-sharp knife across the packaging covering the potent cocaine. He pulled the wrapper open and stuck the knife inside. He pulled it out covered with cocaine. He sniffed it all off from one end of the blade to the other.

"Nobody tells me when I've had enough, whore. I tell you when you have had enough." That was the last thing he said before kneeling down and flipping the kilo over on her face, smothering her with it like a pillow. Juanita struggled to breathe and was forced to inhale cocaine with her next breaths. She clawed at his wrist and arms trying to make him release his grip, but it was useless. She felt like she was

going to pass out as he whispered to her.

"Now this is a fucking party, bitch."

Juanita let go of his wrist, and her hand bumped into the knife he had cut the kilo open with. She didn't know how much strength she had left in her body, but she grabbed the knife and blindly swung it over her head. Ra'mon was too high to see the knife coming, but he felt it as it plunged in the side of his neck. His grip released instantly, and Juanita finally got the relief she needed. She almost choked on the cocaine as she turned over on all fours, still trying to breathe. Ra'mon was struggling on his feet, holding the knife handle which was the only thing left hanging out of his neck. Juanita hadn't completely caught her breath after almost throwing up, but her adrenaline and the cocaine were running through her veins and had woken up her inner beast.

"I'm a Calderon, punta!" she said with her cocaine-covered face before charging at him like a linebacker. She wasn't as big as him, but his current condition made it easy to drive him backward until his back hit the bathroom wall, and he slid down it. Juanita was like a woman possessed as she straddled him. She grabbed the knife handle from his weak grip and snatched the knife out of his neck sending blood spraying everywhere. Ra'mon tried to stop the blood from coming out of the gaping hole with his hands but it was useless as blood continued to seep through his fingers. Juanita's rage was one she didn't know was inside her, and she found herself plunging the bloody knife in his face over and over until he was almost unrecognizable and was barely breathing. She sat on him, breathing heavily with

blood speckles across the cocaine that covered her face.

"When I say you've had enough, you've had enough, punta!" she said before driving the knife down in his throat with both hands. She held it and pushed down with every ounce of energy left in her body until his body stopped convulsing, and he lay still. She was almost in a trance looking at Ra'mon's dead body until she heard something behind her that made her look back, only to see her thirteen- and eleven-year-old sons and her eight-year-old daughter, Marisol, with tears in her eyes. She could still hear her daughter saying, "Mama," holding her hands out for her. Ms. Calderon was so deep in thought she didn't realize it was really her daughter calling her as she came back in her office, snapping her back to reality.

"Mama, you okay?"

"Yes, yes, I'm fine, sweetheart. What's wrong?"

"Nothing. I just wanted to say thank you, and I love you," Marisol said before hugging her with all her might.

"I love you too, *mija*," she said, holding her close. Marisol went right back out the door as quickly as she had come in it. Ms. Calderon made a cross motion with her hand, putting her blessing over her daughter, knowing she was sending her back out with the sharks. Even though she couldn't prove it yet, she knew Ra'mon's family had something to do with the death of her sons and her daughter ending up in jail. She knew they had always suspected she had killed him, especially since he had disappeared without a trace. The only thing she had told them was that he got drunk, high, and ran off in a rage. Twenty years later, she was still sticking to her story. A devilish grin crossed her face as she got ready to inflict her revenge . . . whether or not they were behind it.

***

The next few days were frantic for Tay Tay and her family with the pressure of wondering if her sister was going to pull through. It was weighing down on everyone, not to mention she needed a plan to move the product she was going to be getting in a few days. She was happy when Marisol called her and told her she wanted to go to dinner. Even though she wasn't prepared, she needed some air and Sa'vere and Snoop assured her that they had everything under control while she was away.

Tay Tay had been to many high-class restaurants but none like the one called the Cité on seventieth floor of the North Lake Shore Drive skyscraper. The nighttime view across Chicago was almost as breathtaking as the tight-red Givenchy dress she had on that matched her hair and the soles of her shoes. It only took a second to hear a familiar voice.

"Tay Tay, over here, chica," Marisol said, coming her way. Tay Tay had never seen Marisol made up before, and she found herself staring as she approached. She could see she wasn't the only one staring at Marisol's thick thighs that were barely covered in a tight black skirt.

"Hey, girl. I'm sorry I'm late, I couldn't find anywhere to park," Tay Tay said, hugging Marisol.

"It's okay. Come on, I got a surprise for you."

"A surprise?" Tay Tay said, looking surprised already.

"Yeah, come on," Marisol said excitedly as she took Tay

Tay by the hand and guided her through the restaurant. Tay Tay had to do her best not to just stare at Marisol's phat ass. The private area had the best view of all, but that wasn't what got Tay Tay's attention. It was the pretty blonde sitting at the table that she almost didn't recognize at first.

"Oh my God, Becky!" Tay Tay screamed, running toward Becky.

"Tay Tay!" Becky said, trying to hold her pink skirt down as she got up before giving Tay Tay a hug like family members whose loved one just got out of prison after a long prison term.

"Girl, look at you. Looking like a damn movie star."

"Thanks, Tay Tay. But look at you, bitch, looking like a diva."

"Yeah, you right, bitch, I can't argue with that," Tay Tay said, posing like the paparazzi was around.

"Oh my God, I can't believe we are all free!" Marisol said, hugging both the females at the same time. The women were happy they were all free and together. The hug lasted for a minute until they heard a noise behind them that got their attention. Waiters came in with all types of food and drinks. Within minutes, the tables were covered with steaks and seafood like a buffet.

"This ain't no County Jail's finest cuisine here. Y'all hungry or nah?" Marisol asked.

"Hell, yeah!" Tay Tay and Becky said in unison, ready to enjoy the five-star meal. The ladies ate, drank, and talked for the next thirty minutes, enjoying each other's company, especially since the last meal they shared came out of a

Doritos bag in their jail cell.

"Damn, I ain't ate like that in forever," Tay Tay said, putting her fork on a plate that had nothing left on it but the shell of a lobster tail.

"Who you telling? I been working so much, I sure ain't had time to eat like this," Becky said.

"Where you working, girl?" Marisol asked, still eating.

"I been doing some escorting."

"Escorting?" Marisol asked, surprised.

"Hell, yeah. I been working for this service that hooks me up with high-end clients. Shit, some nights I make 3,000 for just talking to a man about his problems."

"Well, at least you a high-class ho, chica," Marisol said, making them laugh.

"Shut up, you always talking shit, bitch."

"You know what . . . This might be what we need, Marisol," Tay Tay said, looking like a lightbulb had just come on in her head.

"A high-end hooker?" Marisol asked.

"Something like that. You see, what I know is that this bitch here can open up some doors that we can't."

"Y'all losing me," Becky said, looking confused.

"What I'm saying is those high-end clients are who we need to be dealing with, and you got the complexion for the connection. Not to mention, we can use it as a business front to hide the drug money."

"So, y'all back to being Trap Queens is what y'all saying. Ain't that what had y'all in jail in the first place?"

"You damn right, and if they want to stop this money train, that's what they gonna have to do again," Tay Tay said before killing her glass of Hennessey.

"You know what, chica, I think you on to something. Becky, you trying to get down with your girls, or what?"

"Fuck yeah, bitches. I ain't got shit to lose and everything to gain."

"Good, bitch, we 'bout to have a drink for you graduating."

"Graduating from what?"

"From being a high-class ho to the first white Trap Queen."

"I'll toast to that," Tay Tay said, pouring herself another drink before holding her glass up for the toast.

"Y'all bitches ain't shit," Becky said, holding her glass up as well. "To our future . . . May it bring us too much money to count."

"You damn right," Tay Tay said as the girls toasted their glasses, solidifying their new business relationship. Becky was all smiles, and Tay Tay's mind was already racing trying to figure out how to set the operation up. The only one who had mixed emotions was Marisol. Even though she was smiling on the outside, happy for a second chance at the drug game, she was still hurting on the inside, especially after what happened to her the last time. She quickly poured herself another shot and slammed it down, trying to blur the memory that haunted her day and night, but it was no use. She couldn't do anything but shake her head as the tragic night played through her mind like a rerun of *Martin.*

Growing up and being like the drug queen-pin her mother was had always been a dream of Marisol's just like a young boy that wanted to walk in his father's footsteps. Her two older brothers that had been running the Calderon Cartel's operation in the United States were against their mother sending her there to be a part of the family business. But with Marisol's eagerness to get involved regardless of how her brothers felt, and her mother's final say-so, Marisol was given the opportunity to prove she was a true Calderon.

Marisol's brothers, Tito and Victor, had done their best to keep Marisol's involvement in the operation just enough to please their mom at first, but Marisol proved to be an asset, especially when it came to counting the money and keeping the distribution organized. Once they saw her work, they finally accepted her in the operation, and she rarely got a break after that.

"Damn, Marisol, what the fuck. We gonna be here all night already," her tattoo-covered brother named Tito said.

"Shut up, fool, I'm almost done," she replied, feeding the money counter a stack of bills as she sat at the kitchen table of one of their many stash houses.

"Y'all always arguing. Both of y'all should shut up."

"Fuck you, Victor!" Marisol said to her other brother who was standing there in his expensive black suit, looking like the boss he was. Victor was the oldest and ran most of the business while Tito was the muscle. Now with Marisol, they were running full circle. Marisol was putting the last stack of money in the counter, ready to wrap it up for the night, when they heard a knocking at the front door of the house.

"Who the fuck is that?" *Victor asked, especially since nobody knew their location outside of the three people in the kitchen. As soon as the words left his lips, something came smashing through the kitchen window.*

"Get down!" *Tito yelled as he tackled Marisol out of her seat right before the flash bang went off. The noise was defining, but it didn't stop Tito from crawling to the cabinet under the sink as fast as he could and opening it. He didn't hesitate to grab one of the four Draco AK47 handguns and sliding one across the floor to Victor and one to Marisol. Marisol had just grabbed the gun when the kitchen door got kicked in. The assailant in all black with a black ski mask covering his face took aim right at Marisol as she tried to cock the gun.*

"Die, punta!" *Tito yelled before squeezing the trigger of the gun, letting bullets spit from the seventy-five-round drum on the bottom of it. The assailant never got the chance to get off a shot at his sister. The bullets sent him flying into the same door he had just kicked in. Marisol cocked the gun and squeezed the trigger as she saw another assailant appear where her brother had just chopped one down. The first bullet missed, but the second one hit him in his chest followed by four more that she squeezed off in fear.*

The back door was nothing but a distraction as the front door came flying open after being kicked in. Victor had already gotten to his feet and sent bullets flying in the direction of the ones that had kicked it in. He hit two of them, but the third one caught him with machine-gun fire as his gun jammed, sending him smashing into the table

Marisol was next to. Marisol couldn't believe what she had seen and froze, but her brother, Victor, knocking the table over with his bullet-riddled body, is what saved her. The bullets from the back door bit into the table barely missing her head. Marisol and Tito's hearts filled with revenge as their eyes connected after seeing Victor lying there dead. They both started shooting back with no mercy in both directions at the assailants that appeared at the front and back doors. Within seconds, they had six bodies stretched out dead. Silence and gun smoke filled the air and Marisol and Tito held their guns, ready to let off some more rounds. Seeing their brother dead, full of bullets, lying between them, hit like a ton of bricks that sent both of their souls shattering into pieces. Next thing they knew, flash bang grenades seemed to come through the kitchen window and the front of the house like it was raining metal.

"Fuuuuuuuuck, get down, sis!" Tito yelled, but it was too late as the flash grenades began popping off like fireworks on the Fourth of July. The explosions were blinding and deafening. The small explosions and Tito's gunfire made it sound like a war in Iraq. Tito was a soldier for his family and was willing to die for them. His fate was promised as bullets riddled his body from front to back as he continued to shoot until he was lying dead on top of his brother, Victor. Marisol's ears were ringing, and she couldn't even hear herself scream seeing both of her brothers' bloody dead bodies next to her. She didn't care if she died with them as she lay on their bodies, begging them not to die. Within seconds, she felt the barrel of a rifle right before she was snatched off her brothers' bodies by her

hair.

"Noooooo!" she screamed, trying to get back to them, but the assailant with a suit on and a mask squeezed his M-16 clip into their bodies. Marisol broke free and ran into the back of the man, but he just gave her an elbow, knocking her on her butt. She was woozy as he turned around and looked down at her from beneath his mask.

"Fuck you, punta!" she said, spitting blood from her mouth on to his expensive shoes. The last thing she remembered was his sinister laugh and what looked like an owl tattoo on his wrist before he hit her on the head with the butt of his rifle, knocking her unconscious.

Next thing she knew, she was waking up in a hospital handcuffed to the bed, considering the assailant planted kilos of dope next to her and her brothers' dead bodies. She played the police like she was a hooker caught up in the mix and gave them her dead father's last name of Salazar instead of Calderon.

Marisol had sat in the county jail for a couple of months before they dropped the charges. She hated thinking every day about her brothers' deaths and failing her mother. The only bright light she had was Becky and Tay Tay; so to be there with them now, talking about getting into the dope game together, took things to a whole new level. She was ready for whatever, she thought to herself, wanting revenge and redemption almost more than her next breath. She didn't even tell her mother about the tattoo because she wanted the ones responsible for herself. She was deep in thought and almost didn't hear Tay Tay speaking to her, bringing her back to reality.

"Marisol, you okay, girl?"

"Yeah, yeah, I'm good, girl, that drink went down wrong."

"Whatever, bitch. Let me find out you came home and Oscar got you pregnant," Becky said.

"I fucking wish. He's still deported, trying to get back in the country. I'm going to see my husband this week, though, and I just might be pregnant when I come back, so we better make sure we drink all we can tonight," Marisol replied, making them laugh as she took a shot straight from the Hennessey bottle on the table knowing there was no turning back now.

***

"Hey, now, who's that star?" Sa'vere said, sitting at Tay Tay's mother's kitchen table drinking Hennessey with her brother, Snoop.

"Oh, nigga, you know me," Tay Tay replied, smiling as she came and sat on his lap.

"Here y'all go," Snoop said, shaking his head with a smile on his face. He didn't like anybody that liked his sister, but he had never seen her as happy as she was now. So as far as he was concerned, Sa'vere was now his brother.

"Where's Mama?"

"She's in her room, asleep. She done drank some of this Hen to calm down."

"Good, I was hoping she got some rest. Shit, I need a couple of shots too," Tay Tay said, getting up off of Sa'vere's lap to grab her a glass.

"Doctor said it's still up in the air with little sis. I can't believe this shit still. Somebody's gon' pay for this shit on everything."

"Hell, yeah! They definitely gon' pay," Sa'vere said, giving Snoop some dap. Tay Tay couldn't do anything but shake her head knowing their words were true. Having two goons by her side that loved her unconditionally was more than a blessing, she thought, pouring herself a drink.

"Well, let's talk some business. I think I got a way to get us paid heavy. There's only one problem. I need the business startup money, and Wayne's lawyer, Walter, has been avoiding me and shit."

"Oh yeah? How much money we talking?" Snoop asked. "$490,000."

"Shiiiiiiiiiit, we might have to pay this muthafucka a visit. What you think, bruh?" Snoop said, pulling his gun out and setting it on the table.

"I say, nigga, let's do it," Sa'vere replied, pulling his own gun out and setting it on the table as well.

Tay Tay smiled, knowing she had just put some savages on Walter's ass for playing with her and her money.

***

The downtown law office of Walter Shindler was very prestigious like the high-end clientele it attracted. He was not only a lawyer, but also one of Wayne's main drug suppliers. He moved dope through the same rich clients he protected.

He was sitting at his expensive desk when his secretary buzzed in. "Mr. Shindler, I have a couple of new clients out here. They say it's regarding a murder case and they have a retainer."

"Well, send them in!" Mr. Shindler said excited, considering his retainer fee was $100,000. Within seconds, his blond secretary opened his office door, showing the two clients inside. Mr. Shindler's clients were mostly white, so when he saw the two thugs in expensive suits walking in, he was surprised, but he wasn't about to turn down $100,000. He got up to greet the gentlemen.

"Hi. How you doing? I'm Walter Shindler, but you can call me Walter. I hear you've got a problem."

"Yeah, something like that," Snoop said.

"Well, sit down, gentlemen, and tell me what's going on. Can I get you a drink or something?" Walter asked, pointing toward the bar.

"Maybe later; we really want to get down to business. Time is kind of an issue," Sa'vere said as he and Snoop took a seat.

"No problem. Tell me what's going on. My secretary said it's something to do with a murder."

"Yeah, well, that actually depends on you. You see, this murder can actually be prevented, but it all depends on how fast you can come up with $490,000," Snoop said with a straight face. His words hit Walter like a ton of bricks.

"Wait a minute, what's this? Some type of shakedown or something? You tell Taylor she's gonna get her money real soon."

"First off, you need to watch your fucking tone, muthafucka. We ain't here for rain checks," Sa'vere said, pulling out his gun and cocking it.

"Hold up a minute. You can't just kill me in here. You won't ever get out without being recognized, so like I said, gentlemen, tell Taylor she'll get her money soon. Now, see your way out. I have real work to get to."

Sa'vere and Snoop laughed as Snoop pulled out a flip phone from his jacket pocket and dialed a number. As soon as someone answered, he slid the phone across the desk.

"You might want to take that call. It's for you," Snoop said. Walter looked at the phone confused before putting it to his ear and speaking.

"Hello?"

"Daddy, please help us. They've got me and Mom!" Walter's sixteen-year-old daughter said before the phone went dead. Walter just held the phone like he had frozen in time.

"Now, like we were saying, the murder case depends on you," Snoop said, knowing his little goons that had kidnapped Walter's wife and daughter would kill for him without a second thought.

"Okay okay okay, just give me a second. I'll get you your money."

"See, I knew you would see things our way," Sa'vere said with a devilish grin as Walter picked up his phone and dialed a number. It didn't take but a few seconds before he began speaking into the phone.

"Phil, I need you to get off your ass and bring me $500,000 right the fuck now. I'm talking like within the next fifteen minutes, your nerdy fucking ass needs to be walking through that door!" Walter said before hanging up on his accountant and underling.

Fourteen minutes later, a nerdy white man in suspenders and glasses came walking through the door with a black duffle bag filled with $500,000 in hundred-dollar bills. Phil didn't ask any questions when he saw the two thugs in suits. He just gave his boss the bag.

"I'm sorry to keep you gentlemen waiting. Please tell Taylor I'm sorry for the delay. I put an extra $10,000 in for the inconvenience. I hope we're all good?"

"Yeah, we're all good, Walter. Nice doing business with you," Sa'vere said, taking the bag from the man before he and Snoop walked out.

Tay Tay had been sitting in the black Chrysler 300 waiting on her brother and Sa'vere. She was almost ready to go busting in when they got in the car.

"Damn, what took so long? Y'all got my nerves all bad and shit," she said, hitting her Newport as she pulled off from the curb.

"What you mean, what happened, boo? We went in there and walked out with $500,000. Ain't that right, bruh?" Sa'vere said from the backseat, leaning on the bag of money with a smile on his face that Tay Tay could see in the rearview mirror.

"You damn right, bruh!" Snoop said, giving Sa'vere some dap over his shoulder. Tay Tay knew she was surrounded by savages. She didn't even want to know what they had done to get Walter to come off the money. She was just happy they did.

***

"Damn, Wayne, is you gonna answer your damn phone?

It's been ringing for two days," Mesha said as she walked through the Atlanta suite in her T-shirt and panties.

"That ain't nobody but J Mo, and he don't want shit. I told them I'm unavailable until Monday. I'm not interrupting our honeymoon for nobody."

"Well, I'm about to interrupt it because we're out of ice," Mesha said as she walked over to Wayne with the ice bucket.

"Of course, Mrs. Washington," Wayne said, hugging his new bride before taking the ice bucket.

"Oh, yeah, and go see if I left my phone in the car."

"You sure you don't have it? I could've sworn you were on your phone last night."

"Nigga, if I had it, I wouldn't be asking. Damn, Wayne, I always gotta ask you twice for stuff. I bet Tay Tay didn't."

"I'm sorry, Mesha, I just thought—"

"That's the problem, boo, I didn't ask you to think, I asked you to go to the car and get my fucking phone."

"Yes, baby, I gotcha," Wayne said, grabbing his shirt and keys, headed to the car that was in the parking garage.

When the room door closed, Mesha went to her purse and pulled out her cell phone, then scrolled to a number and pressed SEND. It only took a few seconds for J Mo to answer.

"Well, about fucking time you called. While y'all on a fucking honeymoon, shit's going crazy out here in the streets."

"What's going on?"

"First off, I think that nigga, Sa'vere, is behind hitting

Big Ted."

"Why you say that?" Mesha asked like she hadn't put Trell and Sa'vere onto the lick on Big Ted. They were supposed to rob them, and then Trell was going to kill Sa'vere, but she hadn't heard from Trell since.

"Because him and another nigga just walked into Walter's office and made him give them the $500,000 Wayne owed Tay Tay."

"You gotta be fucking kidding me. If you wouldn't have fucked up the hit, none of this would be happening."

"Trust me, we gon' get they asses. I just need you to call your peeps and see if he can push that order up. We need to get back like yesterday."

"Okay, let me see what I can do. I'll be back in a couple of days for some of that dick."

"Good, 'cause I'm gonna dick the shit out of you for getting loud with me over this phone."

"I know, that's why I did it," Mesha said, giggling sensually before hanging up. Her mood quickly changed, thinking about Tay Tay getting the money that she and Wayne had decided not to give her. She didn't know what Tay Tay and Sa'vere were up to, but she wasn't going to stop coming after them until they were dead. There was room for only one queen in this game, and she was gonna make sure nobody came for her throne.

"I'm Mrs. Washington now, bitch," Mesha said, thinking out loud as she wiggled her fingers making the light dance off the six-carat diamond wedding ring Wayne had given her.

***

With her nephew's funeral coming up and trying to secure a location for the business front, Tay Tay had convinced Marisol to have her mother hold off with the load until they secured the location. Even with her nephew and sister weighing heavy on her heart, Tay Tay and Marisol looked like bosses as they stepped off the elevator and into the 5,200-square-foot penthouse that occupied the fifty-seventh floor of The Heritage Building at Millennium Park.

"Welcome, I'm Scarlet," said the white, redheaded freckle-faced woman as she approached.

"Hi, I'm Taylor, and this is my friend, Marisol. I hope we're not late."

"No, you're not late at all," Scarlet said, shaking Tay Tay's and Marisol's hand. She couldn't help but check both ladies out wondering how they got their designer Gucci dresses that weren't even out yet.

"Well, that's good. I was trying to find a parking spot forever. I guess that will change if we get this place."

"That's true, but this place is $5.25 million and requires a hefty deposit and thorough background check," Scarlett said like she was trying not to waste her time.

"Well, are you gonna show us the place or not?" Tay Tay said, trying not to snap.

"Yes, of course. Right this way," Scarlett said as she started the tour. "This unit features tall ceilings with floor-to-ceiling windows that offer an unobstructed view of Millennium Park and Lake Michigan," Scarlet said with a dry voice as she turned around to make sure they were following. Tay Tay had to grab Marisol's arm to keep her from choking Scarlet from the back. Tay Tay knew they needed this place. It was high-end property that matched the kind of clients they were looking for, especially since most of them lived in the building already. She couldn't help but think of the Carter Building from the movie *New Jack City*, where Nino Brown took over a black housing project and ran it like a Fortune 500 crack house. She planned on doing the same thing here.

Throughout the fifteen-minute tour, Tay Tay tried to figure out the redhead's weakness, knowing her accounts were still under siege. A background check would make her look like a drug dealer right now. Just as they were nearing the end, Scarlet excused herself for a second to answer her phone. She thought she was out of ear's reach, but Tay Tay had learned to ear hustle on Wayne over the years of her dysfunctional marriage and zoned right in on the conversation like the FBI.

"Scott, what the fuck! Just take the money out of the dresser. I'll call you back. I'm with a client!" Scarlet said, hanging up on her cheating-ass husband that made a living off of her and her father's real estate dynasty which owned the building she was showing right now. She quickly turned her attention back to Tay Tay and Marisol, trying to see if they had overheard. Tay Tay did but was playing it off.

"You know what? We appreciate your time. We're going to do a little shopping around, but we'll be in touch real soon," Tay Tay said.

"You sure you don't want to do the application now?" Scarlet asked with a sarcastic tone.

"Yes, we're sure but thanks, though," Tay Tay said, tugging Marisol by her arm who could have killed Scarlet right there on the spot. She didn't say anything until the Penthouse elevator doors closed.

"I could kill that white punta. She don't know who the fuck we are."

"Exactly," Tay Tay said with grin on her face. She had a plan, Marisol could see it in her girl's smile.

***

Scarlet had had a long day full of headaches. First, Scott begs her for money, then promptly disappears; then she has her time wasted by some black and Mexican girls at the penthouse. She had hoped the late-night phone call to see the property paid off. Scarlet had already had several glasses of wine while waiting on her husband to answer the phone when the call came in. She pulled herself together and got there, not just for the money, but because she was bored and intrigued with the man's voice that had called her. She had changed clothes from earlier, especially since she'd heard a man's voice, and men were her best clients.

Scarlet stood there in in her skintight yellow dress that made her look like she was selling herself instead of the property. The elevator doors opening sent her into the role that sold hundreds of properties in the past.

"Welcome. My name is Scarlet. It's nice to meet you!" she said like a new register employee at McDonald's.

"Well, isn't this beautiful."

"Yes, this is a beautiful piece of work. There's over 5,200 square feet of luxury—"

"Nah, I was talking about you, but this view's all right," Sa'vere said, tipping his thousand-dollar Gucci glasses and looking her in the eyes before walking past her toward the huge windows. Scarlet just stood there trying not to blush as she found herself inhaling the essence of his expensive cologne and swag. She pulled herself together before turning around to continue her luxury tour.

"I'm happy you're enjoying the view."

"That I am. I'm hoping to see what else this place has to offer."

"Well, right this way," Scarlet said in a flirtatious tone, continuing the tour. The next five minutes were quiet as Sa'vere followed her while she talked. It wasn't until they got to the luxury bathroom that he spoke.

"Now this is one hell of a shower."

"Yes, it is. It has his and hers showerheads, over twenty jets, surround sound, and LED lighting."

"Lights too? You mind showing me how they work?"

"No problem, that's what I'm here for," she said before walking inside the walk-in shower with Sa'vere behind her.

"This button here controls the lights," she said, pushing the button and making the LED lights turn red.

"Which button? You pressed this one?" Sa'vere said, pressing against her from behind like he was trying to press the button.

"Yesss, that's the one right there," she replied almost melting from feeling him against her. She found herself pushing her ass back wanting to know if the myth was true about black men and their big dicks. She had been cock watching black guys at the gym for years and now here she was alone with one pressed against her little white ass. She knew this was wrong and was about to pull away, but his dick becoming rock hard against her ass made her let out a slight moan as she bit her bottom lip, feeling herself become wetter by the second. She couldn't resist grinding back against his hard dick like a slow jam was playing. Sa'vere pushed her against the wall aggressively like she was about to get a pat down.

"Put your muthafuckin' hands on the wall!"

"Oh shit, I've been a bad girl," Scarlet said, putting her hands on the wall like she was commanded. Her spoiled ass was used to having her own way, and being dominated was a fantasy that her weak-ass husband would never fulfill. His hand grabbed her thigh and slowly made its way up it until it slid her skirt up, uncovering her freshly tanned ass and yellow G-string. His hand found its way to her inner thigh as his lips pressed against her neck. She wanted him to touch her pussy so badly, but he just teased her.

"Please!"

"Please, what, you little fucking white whore. I know what you want. You want to get on your fucking knees and let me shove all this big black dick down your throat. Turn your muthafucking ass around!" Sa'vere said, spinning her around as he began unzipping his pants. His words and the anticipation of seeing a big black dick in person for the first time almost made her come on herself.

"Oh shit!" Scarlet said as she saw Sa'vere's massive dick.

"Oh shit, hell. Get on your knees, you little white whore," he said before slapping her slightly in the face.

"Yes, daddy, yes," Scarlet said, wanting him so badly as she quickly dropped to her knees. Sa'vere wrapped his hand around her red ponytail while he slapped her across her face with his dick with the other hand.

"Open your mouth, bitch!" Sa'vere said, squatting his dick down her throat which she accepted until she almost choked.

"Oh my God!" she said trying to catch her breath, wanting that big black dick back down her throat.

"Don't call God. *I'm* your God, you little white whore," Sa'vere said, smacking her across her face with his dick again.

"Yes, I'm your little white whore."

"I know you are, now get your ass up. I got something special for little whores like you."

"Yes, daddy. Yes, please, let me be your little white whore," she said under his spell like the dick had hypnotized her.

***

Tay Tay almost regretted sending the man of her dreams into the arms of a white woman. The song "Gold Digger" kept playing in her head, especially the part where Kanye West raps, *"And when you get on, he'll leave yo' ass for a white girl."* She knew it was risky, but they needed this building, and she was willing to get it by any means. Tay Tay had taken a shower and threw on a red lace bra that matched her boy shorts and hair. She was looking sexy as ever for Sa'vere when he came in. The thought of her dick in someone else's pussy kind of turned her on. She was admiring her body in the mirror when the sound of the room lock opening instantly got her excited.

"That you, boo?"

"Yeah."

"I'll be out in a second," Tay Tay said looking in the mirror one last time making sure she was looking flawless.

"Take your time." Tay Tay could smell Sa'vere's cologne from the cracked bathroom door and she wanted him now. She walked out of the bathroom. What she saw next made her stop in her tracks. She was even hornier now than she was before she came out of the bathroom.

"Hey, boo, I got company," Sa'vere said with Scarlet on her knees next to him in nothing but her yellow panties and bra.

"Well, what do we have here?" Tay Tay asked with a devilish smile, loving Sa'vere more and more by the second.

"We have a white whore, ain't that right?"

"Yes, daddy, I'm your whore," Scarlet said, loving being dominated.

"Well, little white whore, why don't you crawl over to this bed," Tay Tay said, sitting on the edge of the mattress. Scarlet did as she was told and began crawling toward Tay Tay.

"She's a dirty white whore, and she loves the taste of this black dick," Sa'vere said.

"Oh, is that right? So, you like my big black dick, you little whore? Well, come taste this black pussy, bitch," Tay Tay said, grabbing Scarlet by her red hair with one hand while pulling her panties to the side with the other before forcing Scarlet's face deep into her dripping-wet pussy. Scarlet had never been with a female before, but she licked that sweet black pussy like it was her last meal on earth.

"Yeah, little white bitch, eat that black pussy," Tay Tay said, grinding her pussy all over Scarlet's face, trying to drown her. Tay Tay damn near came in the white girl's mouth thinking about how Scarlet had been looking down on her, and now Tay Tay was doing the same, but with her pussy in Scarlet's mouth.

"Get cho ass up on this bed, bitch, and lie down. You like this black dick and pussy, bitch?"

"Yes, I love it!" Scarlet said, climbing on the bed with her face dripping wet, eating more punishment and loving every second of it.

"Come on, boo, we about to give this white bitch what she wants." Tay Tay didn't hesitate to grab Scarlet by her yellow panties and snatched them off. Sa'vere had rolled a condom on and climbed up on the bed with the two females.

"Open your legs, bitch!" Tay Tay said, pulling her white thighs apart as Sa'vere got in between them.

"Oh shit, you ripping this little white pussy!" Scarlet yelled out as Sa'vere pushed inside her inch by inch.

"Nah, bitch, you wanted this nigga dick, now you gonna get it!" Tay Tay said. Sa'vere showed her cries no mercy as he began beating that white pussy up. Scarlet screamed like she was being killed as Sa'vere continued his assault.

"You love this nigga dick, don't you, white bitch?" Sa'vere said over the sound of his balls slapping against her ass.

"Yes! Yes, I love this dick."

"Bitch, he said *nigga* dick," Tay Tay said, slapping Scarlet in her face.

"Yes! Yes! Yes! I love this nigga dick! Kill this little white pussy!" Scarlet screamed out, saying something she had never said before as her body started shaking frantically. She began squirting gun all over his big black dick. Tay Tay smiled at Sa'vere who had punished the white girl.

"Turn your ass around, bitch. We ain't done with your white ass. You can't handle my dick. Let me show you how it's done." Scarlet turned around on the bed and Tay Tay straddled Scarlet in the sixty-nine position. Tay Tay reached back and snatched the condom off Sa'vere's swollen dick as he took his spot behind her. Scarlet had begun licking Tay Tay's dripping-wet pussy as Sa'vere pushed his big dick inside Tay Tay. Scarlet was like an animal licking Tay Tay's pussy as she watched Sa'vere's dick sliding in and out. Hearing Tay Tay's wetness with each stroke made her want to come again.

"Yeah, daddy, get all this pussy!" Tay Tay said, making Sa'vere go crazy. The dick got so good to her that she had to lick Scarlet's pussy to stop from screaming as she started coming on Sa'vere's dick and Scarlet's tongue at the same time.

"Suck the come off this dick, you little whore," Sa'vere said, pulling his dick out of Tay Tay and shoving it down Scarlet's throat.

"Yeah, that's right, bitch, eat my come off that nigga dick."

Scarlet couldn't fight the orgasms that ripped through her body like never before. Sa'vere plunged his dick back inside Tay Tay and gave her hard strokes as he felt his load rising in his throbbing dick.

"Get all this come, bitch!"

Sa'vere sprayed some of his load inside Tay Tay and the rest all over Scarlet's face.

"Yeah, get all our come, bitch!" Tay Tay said, grinding across Scarlet's tongue and face as she looked back at Sa'vere, loving every inch of her nigga dick.

***

Tay Tay had a long night of drinking and punishing Scarlet with Sa'vere, but it had paid off big time. Scarlet had agreed to get them the Millennium Park Penthouse so long as she could continue being her and Sa'vere's whore. She had also told them that she was down for the business and that she had control over all her father's high-end properties which would expand the business immediately. Now all they were left with was getting the females, Tay Tay thought to herself as she heard the elevator door to the penthouse opening.

"Welcome to Bad and Bougie escort service where we provide high-class services to high-end clients," Tay Tay said as Marisol and Becky stepped off the elevator.

"Bitch, quit playing!" Marisol said, looking around in disbelief. She didn't know what Tay Tay had done to get this place, but she didn't care.

"Wait a minute, y'all, we're really serious about getting in this industry? I mean, I thought you were serious but not this fast," Becky said, looking surprised as well.

"I told you we don't play, chica, ain't that right, Tay Tay?"

"You damn right," Tay Tay said, giving Marisol a high five and hug.

"Damn, I'm all slow and shit," Becky said.

"You right about that slow shit," Marisol said, making them all laugh.

"Fuck you, bitch," Becky replied, giving both of them a hug. This was the first time they had seen Becky since the dinner the three ladies had together when they came up with the escorting idea. Tay Tay and Marisol knew it was up to them to handle the business part of things. Now it was time for Becky to play her role and show them the game.

"Well, now that you see we're about this shit, we need you to give us a crash course on the game," Tay Tay said, ready to get to business.

"A crash course? Y'all have no idea what y'all up against. This game here is one of the oldest professions around—and one of the most cutthroat." Becky couldn't help but to remember what got her started in this lifestyle.

It was her eighteenth birthday and celebrating it was bittersweet for Becky. She had stepped a level closer to adulthood, but the feeling of her parents dying in a freak house fire five months prior still weighed heavily on her heart. Once her parents died, she was forced her to live with her mother's sister in Chicago. Becky had the perfect life until then, full of private schools and anything her heart desired considering she was the only child of a successful drug smuggler for a major Columbian drug cartel. The only thing her parents had left behind was a quarter million in bonds for Becky that she couldn't touch until she was eighteen. Her aunt, Susan, woke her up that morning around eight to make sure they could get to the bank on time to cash her bonds. Her aunt had convinced her that with the business her father was in, the feds might take her money if she left it in the bank, and that she needed to get all her money out. Becky did what she was told. On the way home from the bank, her aunt told her they were stopping at a friend's house for a minute and when they left, they were going to celebrate her birthday. She didn't think anything of it; she was just happy it was her birthday. When they pulled up to the mansion, Becky thought she was staying in the car, but her aunt encouraged her to come in. When they got to the door, her aunt didn't even knock, she just walked inside.

"Surprise! Happy Birthday!" said a dark-skinned man with a Versace shirt on and heavy gold jewelry as they walked in like it was a surprise party, but he was the only one there, and she didn't know him.

"Come on, Becky, say thank you. This is my close friend, Reggie."

"Thanks, Mr. Reggie," Becky said being respectful like she was taught, growing up.

"Just, Reggie, sweetie, me and your auntie go way back. Ain't that right, Susie Q," Reggie said, calling Susan by her nickname.

"That's right, Reggie."

"She told me it was your birthday and that you were new to the area, so you don't have a lot of friends. I told

her I thought we should change all that. Ladies, if you would follow me," Reggie said, taking them both by the hand. Becky loved the mansion, and when they got to the dining room, she was shocked. The room was decorated with birthday decorations with her name, gifts covered the table, and eighteen candles burned on a big birthday cake.

"Happy Birthday, Becky! Go ahead and blow your candles out," her aunt said, walking her niece over to the table.

"I don't know what to say. This is unexpected. But I'm so grateful."

"Trust me, you deserve it. Now make a wish and blow them candles out, sweetie," Reggie said standing next to Becky and Susan. Becky was smiling from ear to ear. She wished she could be this happy forever and blew her candles out. Susan and Reggie clapped.

"Let me take a picture. You're officially eighteen now," Reggie said, pulling out his cell phone. Becky posed as Reggie took multiple photos while she smiled.

"I didn't think I was going to have a surprise party. Oh my God, this is awesome."

"You ain't seen nothing yet. Go ahead, open your gifts," Reggie said, passing her one of the twenty gifts off the table. Becky was like a kid at Christmas for the next ten minutes as Reggie and Susan stood there watching and smiling while she opened clothes and electronics. A lot of the clothes were too provocative for her taste, but she was still grateful.

"Damn, you missed one. Must've fallen in the chair," Reggie said, handing it to her. Becky took the package and

ripped it open. There was a thin Louis Vuitton swimsuit.

"Oh wow," Becky said, blushing.

"Now that's class, niece. You done grew up; now it's time you started dressing like it," Susan said, taking it out of the box and holding it up.

"I don't know about that, Auntie," Becky said giggling, feeling ashamed just thinking of her body in this outfit.

"Excuse me, ladies, where's my manners. Let me get the refreshments. I'll be right back," Reggie said before walking off to the kitchen.

"I hope you're enjoying yourself."

"Of course, Auntie. Thank you."

"Well, don't thank me yet, the party's just starting; trust me. When we leave here, we're gonna go spend some of that money, how 'bout that?"

"I like the sound of that."

Reggie returned with three red glasses, getting their attention.

"I got drinks for everybody. Let's get this party going," Reggie said, passing Susan and Becky a glass. Becky looked at the contents of her glass. It looked like fruit punch, but as she put it to her nose, the potent smell of alcohol made her freeze up and instantly look at her aunt.

"It's okay; it's your birthday, and you're not a baby no more. Shit, me and your mom was partying at sixteen."

"Really?" Becky asked, looking surprised. She had taken a sip of a beer once when she was sixteen with some friends and was scared to come home. Now here she was, and her aunt was giving her approval.

"Have a little fun," Susan said, holding her glass up for

a toast.

"To Becky. May this birthday be unforgettable," Reggie said, holding his glass up. Becky hesitated at first, but the peer pressure and green light from her aunt made her toast with them. She took a sip from her cup and frowned up.

"Yeah, there you go. Trust me, the first sip is always the worst," Reggie said, smiling.

"I hope so," Becky said not wanting another sip, but loved feeling grown. The next thing she knew they hear laughter coming from the kitchen Reggie had just come from. Then in walked a black female and a white female that looked about the same age as Becky. Becky's attention was instantly drawn to them not just because of the red glass in their hands like hers, but because they were dressed in thong bathing suits like the one she had just gotten.

"Is this the birthday girl? Oh my God, she's gorgeous," the black female said.

"Yes, she is. Why aren't you in your bathing suit? This is your birthday party," the dark-haired white girl said.

"Becky, this is Lexus and Brittany. When I told them you were new here and it's your birthday, they wanted to come party with you and show you a good time."

"Thank you," Becky said.

"Don't thank us yet. Come on, girl, the party is waiting on you," Lexus said while her white friend grabbed the bathing suit Becky had just got for her birthday. Becky looked indecisive and glanced to her auntie again for approval.

"Go have fun, Becky. Today all about you, baby," Susan

said.

"I guess," Becky said as the girls grabbed her by her arms and walked her away. Becky hadn't had fun in a while and with her aunt's approval she was game to kick it.

Putting on the bathing suit had Becky all insecure even though her body was flawless and thick for a white girl her age. By the time Lexus and Brittany got her outside, Becky was half a cup in. She couldn't believe the pool party that was going on. There were girls and boys her age everywhere partying like adults. Banners read, Happy Birthday, Becky!

"Come on, girl, this all about you," Brittany said, smiling.

"Hell, yeah, girl, it's your birthday. We gon' do it right in this bitch. Drink up. It's plenty more where that came from," Lexus said, making Becky drink from her glass. Becky had never been drunk, but with each sip, her insecurities were leaving.

"Hey, y'all, it's the birthday girl!" Brittany yelled. The chants of "Happy Birthday, Becky" filled the air. She had never felt like this in her life and the fact that she was damn near naked was a thought of the past. The party went on until about ten o'clock that night. Becky had never had so much fun in her life, and after her parents died, she never thought she would have fun again. She had drunk plenty of liquor and had even let Lexus and Brittany give her a pill to pop, telling her it would help her so she wouldn't get sick drinking. By the time everyone was leaving, Becky was feeling real good and fucked up.

"Hey now, look at the birthday girl," her aunt Susan

said as Lexus and Brittany walked her in the room they had met her in. Becky wasn't even ashamed anymore in front of her aunt and Reggie.

"Hell, yeah, it's my birthday," Becky slurred.

"We'll call you tomorrow, girl," Lexus said.

"Smooches. Happy birthday, girl," Brittany said, making both girls giggle as they left.

"Okay, I'm gonna call y'all!" Becky yelled as she heard the front door close.

"I hope you enjoyed yourself," Reggie said.

"Oh my God, I had such a good time," Becky replied, almost falling into the table.

"Come on, party girl. Let's get you a little rest before we leave. Me and Reggie got some things to talk about," Susan said, putting her arm around her niece.

"Okay, Aunt Susan," Becky replied as her aunt led her away.

Becky could barely remember the walk to the upstairs bedroom, but the luxury bed was like lying on a cloud of pillows.

"I'm so proud of you for being such a grown-up today."

"Thank you, Auntie, for everything." As soon as Susan's words left her lips, the room door opened and in came Reggie.

"Is everything okay? I hope the birthday girl enjoyed herself."

"Oh, she had plenty of fun, ain't that right, Becky?"

"Yes, I had plenty of fun."

"That's good. Having fun and feeling good is what it's all about," Reggie said, sitting on the other side of the bed *next to Becky.*

"Oh, she's a grown-up now," Susan said, pulling the strings loose on the side of Becky's swimsuit. Becky felt the strings coming loose but couldn't move.

"Yeah, she's all grown-up," Reggie said, putting his lips on her pussy that her auntie had just uncovered. Becky was almost numb, but a pleasure she had never felt before seemed to fill her pussy, considering she was a virgin. Becky had looked for her aunt for reassurance all day; now, there she was rubbing her head as her friend, Reggie, feasted on her niece. The last thing Becky remembered from that night was Reggie on top of her with his dick out about to penetrate her for the first time.

The next few days were almost a blur to Becky, especially since she had been fed drugs and liquor like it was food. She didn't remember leaving the bed her aunt had taken her to. The only thing she remembered was glimpses of different men humping on top of her. By the time she came to reality, she was strung out on Oxy and Ecstasy and Reggie was her pimp since her aunt had sold her to him so she could get out of the pimp hand he had on her. Becky never saw a dime of her money and ended up being pimped out by her aunt and Reggie for the last eight years. And the sad part was, after all they did to her, she was still working for them and built breeding escorts from the day they turned eighteen just like they had done her. Revenge had always been on her mind, but she never had the heart to pull it off. Now as she stood there with Tay Tay and Marisol, she felt like it might be a new day.

"Hello? Earth to Becky, is you their bitch? Is you gonna

show us the game or not?"

"Hell, yeah, I'm about to show you this game from top to bottom," Becky said, feeling her opportunity for revenge, hoping to finally break free from Reggie and Susan who had the city on lock. She knew there was danger in this game, but now wasn't the time to tell Marisol and Tay Tay. They would just have to deal with it when the time came.

"Good. For a minute I thought you was backing out," Tay Tay said.

"Never that. I'm in it to win it. Y'all ain't about to get rich without me," Becky said, making them all laugh.

"So, what would be the most important thing in getting started?" Tay Tay asked, ready to get down to business.

"Getting the girls is the key. There's a lot of escort agencies doing numbers because they got the top females working for them. The people I work for are cutthroat and don't like competition."

"Good, 'cause we don't like competition, either," Marisol said, ready for whatever tried to stop them from getting to the top.

"Well, I think I might know where to find the girls," Tay Tay said.

"Where?" Becky asked.

"The same place we all met. There's plenty of females in there looking for a way, and we might be what they need."

"How we gonna get in jail to talk to them?" Marisol asked.

"Leave that part to me. I think I might have someone

that can help with that."

"So, what you want us to do?" Marisol asked.

"Y'all go furniture shopping and turn this into the Bad and Bougie Escort Agency."

"Hell, yeah, shopping is our hobby," Marisol laughed.

"I agree with that," Becky said, giving Marisol a high five.

"Good, we right on track then. Once we get our business account and license, we'll be ready to open our doors," Tay Tay said.

"I love the sound of that. My mother also said she wants to pay for the funeral for your nephew. Any news on your sister?"

"She's day to day; can't do nothing but pray. Tell your mom I said thank you so much."

"I'll tell her."

"I'm so excited we're making this happen. I couldn't ask for two better friends to do this with," Becky said, almost tearing up.

"Awwww," Tay Tay said, hugging her.

"Here y'all go with this mushy shit. You bitches gonna make my mascara run," Marisol said, trying not to get emotional.

"Get over here, bitch," Tay Tay said as Becky and Tay Tay invited her into a group hug which she gladly accepted. Becky hadn't felt sisterhood like this, and she was willing to die to protect the feeling. Going against Reggie and her aunt Susan was like playing Russian roulette, but she knew she could handle them with her sisters beside her.

***

While Tay Tay was handling business, Sa'vere had business of his own to get to. He had gotten used to the cushy life Tay Tay had made him a part of, but there was no place like home. He closed his room door of the raggedy East Side Motel 6. He had called this home for the last ten years since he hit the streets on his own after his mother died. His mom was a prostitute in the area and strung out on heroin which was how he knew all the junkies, and all the junkies knew him. Tay Tay may have had the business side, but he was A-1 in the trap and planned on proving it. He was getting ready to turn on the TV when he heard a knock at the room door. Sa'vere pulled his gun out of his waistband and cocked it.

"Who is it?" he yelled, but there was no response. Then, whoever it was, knocked again. Sa'vere made his way toward the door ready to kill anything moving before they killed him. He held the gun up to the door as he peeped through the peephole cautiously. When he saw who it was, he almost wanted to pull the trigger, but his mother would roll over in her grave if he did. He hesitated to open the door for a second, but she began knocking again.

"Nigga, open this damn door and quit playing with me!"
Sa'vere shook his head before opening it.

"Pam, I got shit to do."

"Whatever. You ain't got shit to do. Damn, can't I come check on my little brother," Sa'vere's sister said with a mink coat and glasses on, looking like a baller's wife.

"You ain't checking on me. What you want? I told you I got shit to do."

"Oh, nigga, I'm checking on you because your dumb ass out here doing stupid shit about to get killed."

"Fuck is you talking about?"

"Oh, you know what the fuck I'm talking about, Sa'vere. You and Trell's ignorant ass out here robbing niggas and shit. I'm surprised he ain't here with you."

"Like I said, I don't know what you talking about. I ain't seen that nigga Trell in months. That nigga, Ted, probably saying that shit because we got into it. I done heard the rumors."

"Whatever, Sa'vere. Ain't this the same shit that got Mama killed? You ain't learned shit!"

"That shit wasn't my fault."

"Nigga, you were the one out there robbing people, then bullets flying through our window. Shit, they sure wasn't looking for me."

"They were probably looking for that sucka-ass nigga Red Man."

"Nigga, leave my husband out of this shit. Didn't that nigga look out for us and keep us eating when Mama died? Now, here you go throwing dirt on his name. I swear I don't know why I even give a fuck about you. Shit, Red Man trying to save your ass from the people you robbed. This shit's bigger than Ted. You hit Red Man's plug. Now he stuck in the middle of your shit."

"Well, you or him don't do me no favors. Like I said, I don't know what the fuck you talking about, and I got shit to do, so if you done, hit the door."

"You a stupid-ass nigga. You gon' fuck around and get killed over that bitch, Tay Tay or Taylor, whatever the dick her name is. I ain't got money to be burying your stupid ass over some pussy. What's wrong with you, nigga? You used to run bitches, not let bitches run you. You better wake the fuck up and come get with your blood. I'm sure if you come work for Red Man, he can get you outta this shit you in."

"I'm good. Shit, tell that nigga I'm gon' have a job for him in a minute."

"I guess, nigga. Just know if I can find you, *they* can find you."

"Shit, I ain't never said I was hiding. Muthafucka looking for me, I ain't hard to find. Now have a nice day, sis." Pam rolled her eyes at her brother and stormed out, slamming the room door behind her.

She was heated at her brother as she got into her white-on-white SL 500 Mercedes-Benz. She knew her brother had always been stubborn and wild. Burying her mother and having to make sure she and her brother were straight wasn't easy. She was four years older than Sa'vere, and Pam had always acted like Sa'vere's mother considering their mom's heroin and crack habit. She knew they were like oil and water, but Sa'vere was her heart, and in Pam's eyes, she always had her brother's best interest at heart, even when he didn't know it. She pulled out her iPhone and dialed a number as she got in her car.

"Shaqauna, hey, bitch, I need you."

"What's up, girl?" Pam's best friend said through the phone.

"We gon' have to do some investigating."

"Red Man cheating, bitch?"

"Nah, ho, I'd kill his ass. This about Sa'vere. It's some raggedy-ass bitch got him caught up in all types of bullshit, and you know I don't play about my brother."

"I already know, bitch. What you want to do?"

"We gon' find this bitch. Her name's Tay Tay. She from out West."

"Don't trip, bitch, I'm on it."

"Fasho. We still going out tonight?"

"Hell, yeah."

"Good, I'll hit you later. Let me know what you find out."

"A'ight, bitch, I got you." Pam hung up the phone with a devilish grin on her face. She knew if anybody could find out your business, it was her best friend Shaqauna.

"My brother ain't 'bout to die behind no pussy," Pam said, thinking out loud as she pulled out of the parking lot.

Chapter 7

Shit Just Hit the Fan

Tay Tay had tried to keep herself busy as much as she could, but she knew the reality of her nephew's funeral was coming, whether or not she wanted to accept it.

The funeral was beautiful, and his closed casket had SpongeBob airbrushed on it with flowers that matched since it was Jabari's favorite. Seeing her mom broken down was the hardest for Tay Tay, but she did her best to stay strong. She couldn't help but feel responsible for her nephew's death. Sa'vere had done his best to convince her otherwise, but forgiving herself was going to take some time. She was just happy she had a strong man like Sa'vere by her side, she thought to herself, as they came out of the church hand in hand. The limos were waiting for them and the family so they could go to the grave site. The sound of screeching tires and police sirens got everybody's attention. Plainclothes detectives hopped out of the cars with guns drawn. It didn't take Tay Tay long to recognize Detective Conan, especially since he was coming their way.

"What the fuck do you want now with your crooked ass?" Tay Tay said.

"This is a damn funeral, goddammit, and y'all need to respect it," Ms. Brown said, having to be held back by Snoop.

"Well, I'm sorry for the inconvenience, but Sa'vere Montgomery, we need you to come with us for questioning."

"For what?"

"For a homicide and home invasion," the detective said, nodding for his officers to cuff him.

"This is some bullshit!" Tay Tay yelled at the officers.

"It's cool, baby. I ain't did shit."

"Whatever. I hear this shit all the time. Take him away. You have a nice day, Tay Tay," Detective Conan said, laughing as they walked away.

"Oh my God, Mama!" Snoop yelled as the stress got the best of Ms. Brown, and she passed out on the church steps. Tay Tay's heart shattered into a million pieces as she ran to her mother's side.

"Someone get an ambulance!" she yelled in a panic.

"I'm calling right now!" Marisol said. Tay Tay's lawyer, Nicole, was just coming out of the church chatting with the pastor, unaware of what was going on outside until now.

"Oh my God, what's going on?" Nicole said running toward Tay Tay.

"Please, go get my man! We got this!" Tay Tay said with tears running down her face.

"Okay, okay!" Nicole replied, trying not to panic as streams of tears ran down her face. She didn't know what was going on, but she was about to find out. She walked down the church stairs in her six-inch heels, trying not to fall.

***

The interrogation room didn't have anything in it but three chairs and a steel table with a mirrored window so someone could watch from the other side. Sa'vere had been handcuffed to the table for about thirty minutes before the interrogation room door opened and in walked Detective Conan and a dark-skinned detective.

"I'm Detective Conan, and this my partner, Detective Watts."

"I know who the fuck you are."

"Well, good, then you know why the fuck you're here then!" Detective Watts said, taking a seat at the table with a folder in his hand.

"Actually, I don't, and whatever y'all want to talk about, I wish y'all would get it over with. I got shit to do."

"Oh, you think this shit's a game? We got a drug house with dead bodies in it, and the word is, you and this man here did it!" Detective Watts said, pulling out a photo of Trell.

"Who the fuck is that?" Sa'vere said, picking up the photo and looking at Trell like he was a stranger.

"Now, see, you're testing our intelligence, Sa'vere. And I hate when people play with my intelligence. This is your best friend. Y'all have been arrested together over ten times going back to juvie. See, the funny thing is, the last time his family saw him alive was the day of the home invasion.

Now he just happens to be missing, but you're not," Detective Conan said.

"You know what I think?"

"What?" Detective Watts asked.

"I think y'all should spend your time trying to find a missing person instead of blowing smoke at me. If you did your homework, then you know I'm cut for this jail shit. You either prove what the fuck you're saying, or let me go. Either way, you gon' have to do your fucking job."

"This shit's bigger than some bodies in a crack house. You playing games with the wrong fucking people. And one thing you need to know is, these are *my* fucking streets," Detective Conan said, heated.

Sa'vere didn't say anything, but his nonchalant look spoke volumes. A knock at the mirrored glass got the detective's attention and broke the tension in the air.

"I'll be right back," Detective Conan said to his partner as he walked out of the room. He entered another room where they could see inside the interrogation room.

"He's not gonna budge. He's way too smart to tell on himself or give the shit back. We can't even hold him but seventy-two hours."

"Well, he can't leave here then," Wayne said, staring at the man who was fucking his now ex-wife and had robbed their operation.

"How am I gonna do that?"

"I pay you to figure shit out, not to ask me questions, Detective. I mean, unless you don't want your next payment," Wayne replied.

"Just cool out, I got this shit."

"I knew I could count on you, Detective," Wayne said, walking out of the room. Detective Conan hated Wayne's arrogant attitude and would rather deal with J Mo, but he worked for both of them and wasn't about to mess up the hearty payment he received for him and his unit of corrupt cops. Conan and his drug unit had made a mighty good living keeping the heat off Wayne and J Mo, knocking out any competition that got in their way.

"Fuck me!" Detective Conan said, thinking out loud as he stormed out of the room knowing his job had just gotten a little harder.

***

Tay Tay was nearly drained from the day and didn't know how she kept herself going. Her mother had suffered a mild stroke, and she still had no word on Sa'vere. She had called Nicole several times, but her phone was just going to the voice mail.

After getting her mom settled in her hospital room, Tay Tay made her way to her sister's room. She hadn't been there in a couple of days mainly because she hated seeing her sister like this. She had planned on coming here today anyhow to bring a rose from Jabari's casket, knowing her sister would want one. Seeing Alicia on the breathing machine instantly brought tears to her eyes, even though she told herself she wasn't going to cry.

"Oh my God, Alisha, I swear I'm so sorry for all this. I'm gonna make those responsible suffer, I promise you that," Tay Tay said, kissing her sister on the forehead. She wiped her tears that had fallen on her sister's face before she continued. "I brought you a rose. I'm going to put it in this vase for you. I can't wait till you get out of here, sis. I swear we gon' live it up like we should've been doing. I love you so much, little girl," Tay Tay said, squeezing Alisha's hand. She just stood there, staring at her sister, wishing she would wake up.

A knock at the door got her attention. She was relieved to see it was Nicole, but by the look on her face and the fact that Sa'vere was not with her, she knew she didn't have good news. Tay Tay took a deep breath and wiped the tears from her eyes before heading out to see what Nicole had to say.

"Hey, girl, your brother told me you were down here. What are they saying about Mom?" Nicole said, looking like she was worn out.

"She had a mild stroke. The doctors want to run some tests on her and said it's best that she stays here for a few days. What's going on with Sa'vere? I've been calling you."

"My phone was dead. It took me three hours to even find him. Crooked-ass cops had some of their friends 'lose' Sa'vere's paperwork. By the time I got to him, he had already used his right to remain silent and had both detectives highly pissed off."

"That's my boo. So, what's his bond?"

"Right now, he doesn't have one."

"Why not?" Tay Tay said, getting nervous.

"Calm down. They've got him on a seventy-two-hour hold."

"Meaning?"

"Meaning they ain't got shit on him. They're just buying time. Come Tuesday, he should be a free man. I'll be down at the courthouse ready. I've got a busy schedule this week."

"Now that you say that, I've been meaning to run a little business by you."

"I love business."

"Good, because I'm about to have the grand opening to my escort service next Friday."

"Congratulations, but I'm not an escort. I mean, I'm bad and all, but . . ." Nicole said, making them laugh.

"No, silly. I need your help getting the girls. And for the record, you *are* bad."

"Thanks, girl. Please tell me how I can help you get the women?"

"Looks like you need a cup of coffee. What do you say we go get a cup and talk?"

"I'd say, lead the way."

Tay Tay was hurting, but executing her master plan was all the revenge she needed to start healing.

***

The last twenty-four hours were nothing new to Sa'vere. He had been in and out of jail his whole life since a juvenile. He knew the law, plus Nicole had verified that he could only be held for seventy-two hours. The only witness to the home invasion and the homicides was Trell, and he was no longer breathing. Now, all he had to do was chill until the guard said pack it up.

He was happy when they moved him to a floor where he

was sure to know somebody from the hood. Even though Sa'vere didn't get caught up in the gang stuff growing up, he was still known and respected by many. He looked around the floor he had been taken to, but he saw a bunch of unfamiliar faces. Walking into the two-man cell, Sa'vere could see the scared-looking blond white boy who looked like he had been abused like most of the white boys in the county jail. Sa'vere just put his blanket on the bunk and sat down. He was about to speak to his cell mate but the white boy got up and hurried out of the cell like he was scared for his life. Sa'vere glanced over at the cell door and there was a black male standing there with little braids sticking up all over his head.

"You know you gonna have to pay to stay here, homie."

"Oh, yeah? I didn't get that memo, nigga!" Sa'vere said, standing up. He wasn't about to bow down to anybody, and he had to prove it as the black man came running his way with a shank in his hand.

The man's first swing missed, and Sa'vere made him pay with a blow to the jaw, making him drop the shank and have no choice but to grab Sa'vere to keep from falling. Sa'vere tried to get the man off of him, but another black man with a shank came running in the cell. By the time Sa'vere saw him, he had already been stabbed in the side. Sa'vere felt the pain, but his adrenaline kept him in the fight. When he saw the man about to take another swing, he used all his strength to hold the first man up, using him as a human shield. The man screamed out in pain, taking the shank in the back, forcing his legs to buckle. The second assailant couldn't believe he had stabbed the wrong person and couldn't get his shank back fast enough. Sa'vere rained blows down on him until he was bloody by the toilet. Sa'vere was leaking blood and out of breath as he staggered out of the cell and closed the cell door behind him. The inmates watched on, loving the bloodshed. Sa'vere's vision got blurry, and the last thing he heard was the guards yelling "lock down!" before he fell to the ground and passed out.

***

The courthouse was packed Monday morning just like Nicole said it would be. She usually came in full of confidence. She had used her looks and smarts to get ahead and her double threat had her known as one of the most feared defense attorneys around. She had worked her way to the top and got her own law firm to help all types of people, though mostly drug dealers. Her brother was sentenced to life for drugs, and she made it her goal to fight to get him out and help other drug dealers as well. She had figured out a system to help dealers move drugs back and forth. She knew who was snitching and who was real and worked it to her advantage.

Now here she was about to use her job for something new, especially since it paid well. Normally, she would come in and take care of her paid clients, but today, she was taking cases pro bono like she was a public defender again. One by one, she handpicked females and took their cases. She was looking for pretty women with drug and prostitution charges. She talked to each female about their case and told them she was going to try to get the charges beat, but in the meantime, she would attempt to get them out on bond. The inmates didn't realize that they were really on a job interview. If Nicole thought the female fit the criteria, she told them once they get out that it would look good to have a job, and she could help them with that. She gave them a business card with a phone number on it and told them to call the number when they were released and that she referred them. The females were grateful, especially since most of them had been sitting in jail with a public defender and a bond they couldn't make. Now they had one of the top attorneys around taking their case for free and offering them an opportunity to make some money. The ladies were all smiles, and so was Nicole, considering she was getting a cut of company profits and a $200 finder's fee for each female she recruited. She was skeptical when Tay Tay told her the business, but thirty females later, she was trying to figure out how she could recruit more women in a day. She knew Friday was opening day, and she planned on doing her part for the next week to make it a success.

***

The last seventy-two hours had seemed like forever for Tay Tay. Between her mom still being in the hospital, and her getting the grand opening together, all she wanted right now was a hug from Sa'vere. Tay Tay rode with Nicole to get him out of jail since the time to hold him was up. Nicole had been in the police station for almost two hours before she came walking quickly toward the car. Tay Tay didn't think anything of it, knowing that county took forever to let you free.

"They always taking forever to let people out and shit. I can't stand the county," Tay Tay said as Nicole got in and closed the car door. Nicole stayed silent for a second before speaking.

"Tay Tay, we've got a problem."

"What type of problem?" Tay Tay asked, looking confused.

"They can't release Sa'vere right now."

"Why not? I thought you said he had seventy-two hours. What type of shit they trying to pull?"

"Everything was all hush-hush, but I talked to one of my friends that's a guard. He said there was a stabbing the other day where two people were stabbed. One died, and another man was beaten badly. He said the jail is trying to keep it under wraps until they know exactly what to say to the public since the jail is already under investigation."

"No, Lord, this can't be happening to me! This has got to be some type of sick, fucking dream. My baby ain't dead. I'm just not gonna believe it. He told me he would never leave me, and I know he meant it."

"I know he did too," Nicole said, trying to comfort Tay Tay the best way she could.

"Somebody's gotta tell us something," Tay Tay said, crying.

"Trust me, I'm gonna find out something soon. Right now, you need to get yourself together for the opening and let me handle the rest. No news is good news, and we're just gonna keep believing, girl."

"You're right, he's gonna be okay."

"I'm telling you, they're just trying to protect themselves from a lawsuit. I'm sure Sa'vere's just fine. He's a damn soldier," Nicole said, putting the car in drive, praying her words of comfort came to life. She wondered how Tay Tay had taken so much pain in such a short time and was still ticking.

***

The last week, Becky had been on a mission. Since the meeting with Tay Tay and Marisol, she had taken the new business venture and treated it like her next breath in life. She had stopped going to work and spent her time passing out grand opening cards to some of her personal high-end clients. She even tried to convince some of the females to come with her to the new company. She thought Reggie and her aunt were going to keep calling her, but after the first couple of days of not answering, the phone calls stopped. Becky had been to the beauty shop that morning, getting ready for the opening. Her little taste of freedom made her feel like nothing could stop her, and it showed in her smile as she walked through the door to the condo that escorting had paid for. She had a bunch of outfits to try on for tonight.

Becky was so deep in thought, she missed the person sitting on the couch.

"Well, look at you, even prettier than the day I first laid eyes on you," the smooth voice said, startling Becky and sending a chill down her spine.

"Reggie!"

"Well, at least you still know my name because you sure

done forgot who got you all this."

"I didn't forget. I'm done!"

"You not done, ho. One thing you know I hate is a fucking liar. You thought you could leave me, then turn my loyal hoes against me, and start your own business. I see the apple don't fall far from the tree. Your aunt thought she could leave me once upon a time too. Then I made her kill your fucking parents, give me all your money, and made you one of my number one prostitutes. Bitch, I *own* you!" Reggie said, standing up from the couch. Becky wanted to attack him for what he had just said, but she knew she was no match for his punishment and decided to run toward the kitchen instead. She saw the knives in her knife rack and immediately grabbed the biggest one, knocking the rest to the floor. She turned around, ready to defend herself, but Reggie slapped her across her face as soon as she turned in his direction. The blow knocked her into the counter, making her drop the knife. She couldn't recover before she felt him grabbing her hair with all his strength, messing up her $100 hairdo.

"You thought I was playing when I told you that you mine for life, ho. Well, I'm about to show you who's your daddy, bitch! And when I'm done with your ass, bitch, you owe me for a week's worth of work. And I'm gon' get every dime outta your ass!" he said, pushing her head hard on the counter as he began unfastening his pants. He pulled his dick out and stroked it with his hand, ready to punish her.

"Fuck you!" Becky said, numb after the years of abuse she had suffered at his hands. She didn't even budge as he ripped her panties from under her tight white skirt. Reggie was ready to push inside her ass and break her until she begged him for forgiveness—but a voice caught him off guard.

"Aww, hell, nah, that's my chica!" Marisol said as she saw her friend about to be raped. Reggie had been so caught up in hurting Becky, he hadn't heard anyone come into the house. Marisol came flying across the kitchen and jumped on his back with no regard for her safety. Reggie struggled to hold Becky down and get Marisol off of him, so he chose one, and decided on getting Marisol off of him. He threw her down, and as soon as she hit the floor, he felt a sharp pain in his ribs, but the pain didn't stop him from hitting Tay Tay and knocking her to the floor.

"You bitches want to play? Then let's play!"

"Fuck you, muthafucka!" Becky said before stabbing him in the back with the knife she had dropped. Reggie tried to remove the knife that was deeply embedded in his back, but it was out of his reach.

"Fucking punta!" Marisol said, grabbing a knife off the floor and stabbing Reggie in his lower back as he was losing his balance. Reggie fell to the floor and screamed in pain as he rolled around. The females grabbed knives off the floor and stood over him as he bled everywhere.

"Please call an ambulance—I'm dying!" Reggie pleaded as he tried to crawl across the floor on his stomach like a snake.

"No, bitch, you *already* dead," Tay Tay said as she stabbed him.

Immediately, all three of them went on a stabbing spree

until he was bloody and lifeless. They sat there breathing heavily with blood splattered all over their faces and clothes.

"Oh my God, he's dead!" Becky said, watching the blood seeping from over one hundred stab wounds.

"Fuck that punta. Better him than us!" Marisol said before stabbing him again.

"What are we gonna do? The police ain't trying to hear that," Becky said, looking worried.

"Just calm down a second. Let me get my phone," Tay Tay said, getting up and running to her purse. She had hoped to never have to call this number, but Sa'vere told her to call it if she needed help when he wasn't around. The phone had only rung a couple of times when a voice she recognized answered.

"What's good, Tay Tay? You okay?"

"Big Meat, I need help bad."

"Say no more. Just text me the address."

"Okay," Tay Tay said, hanging up the phone. She quickly texted the address before returning to her girls.

"Everything's gonna be okay, trust me," she said, trying to convince herself as well. In that moment, they all realized they would kill for each other, and what happened today would be taken to the grave. It was blood in, blood out, and they all knew it without having to say a word.

***

As fabulous as Tay Tay, Marisol, and Becky looked as they got off the elevator at the grand opening party, you would've never guessed they had stabbed a man to death earlier that afternoon.

Tay Tay was grateful to Big Meat's loyalty toward Sa'vere. He had gotten rid of Reggie and helped them clean up the crime scene. He had even said he was going to find out what was up with Sa'vere for her.

The ladies were surprised at the turnout, and Scarlet had been behind most of it. She not only got them a rich clientele but had also spent the week fixing the females up like she was on a makeover show. Some of the tenants didn't want that kind of business in the high-class building, but she was a daddy's girl and got what she wanted regardless of who didn't like it. To put the cherry on top, she had turned the vacant properties in the building into dens of pleasure. Some wanted sex, some wanted companionship, while others wanted drugs. Whatever the case, they offered all those services discreetly and in a safe environment where clients didn't have to worry about getting ripped off. The smile on Tay Tay's face was all Scarlet needed to see to know she had done a good job. She just hoped she could be punished for it later, feeling herself getting wet by the second.

The females mingled for the next few hours as guests enjoyed the free food and drinks that they supplied. The women were already putting the pleasure rooms to use with the male guests. Everything was finally feeling like the struggle was all worth it until Tay Tay saw Snoop looking for someone. He was in charge of security and almost looked like a thug-ass Secret Service agent. When they locked eyes, she realized she was the one he was looking for.

"Everything okay, bruh?"

"Hell, yeah, just making sure my sister's okay."

"You know I'm good. Just happy everything is going smoothly, ready to take this business to the next level. Look at all these rich folks."

"Hell, yeah, sis. I ain't never been around this many rich folks in my life."

"How's security going?"

"We ain't got no problems that we can't handle. Had a drunk guy take it too far, but the guys took care of him," Snoop said with a devilish grin. Tay Tay was proud of her brother, and she could tell he was proud also. He was able to hire his goon squad from the block and give them jobs as security, making him the real boss he always wanted to be.

"What y'all two talking about?" Marisol said, all smiles, loving the turnout.

"You," Snoop said.

"Well, that must be why you're smiling then," Marisol replied, flirting back with him.

"Any time you need private security, I'm only a holler away."

"Well, I'll make sure to holler when I need you, papi."

"Oh Lord, y'all are too much for me. That's my cue to check on Becky," Tay Tay said, shaking her head. She really wasn't with her brother talking to her friends, especially the married ones, but she couldn't blame him. Marisol was definitely a bad bitch, and that's the only type of female she could see her brother being with.

Tay Tay had done her best to keep an eye on Becky. After what had happened earlier, Becky had to be going crazy inside. It didn't take long for Tay Tay to spot her at the bar mingling with some man looking like she had too much to drink.

"Excuse me, can I borrow her for a second?" Tay Tay said, interrupting the conversation Becky was having with the gentleman.

"I'll be right back. This is my girl, Tay Tay," Becky slurred as Tay Tay led her away by her arm. Tay Tay walked Becky off to one of the bedrooms that Marisol and Becky had turned into offices.

"You okay, girl?" Tay Tay asked.

"Yeah, I'm good. Life don't get better than this," Becky said, putting a fake smile on that only lasted a few seconds. Then she broke down in tears, and Tay Tay quickly hugged her.

"It's okay, girl. I know you're hurt, but it's gonna be okay."

"I know, Tay Tay. I love you so much."

"I love you too, girl. We all we got."

A knock at the office door got their attention. Becky quickly wiped her tears away.

"Come in."

"Sis, I ain't mean to interrupt you, but there's some females out here who want to talk to you about Sa'vere."

"Where they at?" Tay Tay said, excited to find out something.

"Outside. I'm going to have them sent up." Snoop leaned over his wristwatch. "Send them up," he said into the microphone like the Secret Service.

Five minutes later, the office door opened and Snoop

showed two black females in.

"How you ladies doing? I hear you want to talk about Sa'vere."

"Yeah, I want to talk about him. I don't want you to mess with him anymore."

"*Excuse* me? And who are you?"

"I'm his sister, Pam, and this is my girl, Shaqauna," Pam said, introducing her heavyset friend.

"Well, Sa'vere's a big boy, so I'm sure he can make up his own mind about who he deals with."

"See, that's *my* little brother, and *your* trifling ass got him caught up in some shit that's gonna get him killed. So, before that happens, it's gonna be me and you, ho."

"Bitch, you roll up in here threatening me over a nigga that ain't even brought your name up before. I got a news flash for you, bitch. That's *my* man, *gonna be* my man, and *ain't shit* you or nobody else can do about it."

"Hold up, bitch, who you talking to?" Shaqauna asked, ready to strike, but Tay Tay ended all that when she set the .45 automatic on her desk.

"Now, I'm telling you, bitches, I done had a messed-up-ass day. If I was you, sister-in-law, I'd get you and your pet monster outta my fucking building 'fore shit gets real in this bitch."

"Come on, let's go, y'all. Out of here," Snoop said, taking over before his sister snapped.

"We'll see you later, that's fasho," Pam said as she walked out.

"Maybe at Christmas dinner, bitch!" Tay Tay yelled, getting in the last word. Within seconds, Marisol came into the office and closed the door.

"What's going on?" Marisol said, seeing the females being escorted out and the gun on Tay Tay's desk.

"Supposedly, Sa'vere's sister come to check me about messing with her brother, like we some kids or something."

"Bitch, you gotta be kidding," Marisol said, looking surprised.

"Funny thing, he ain't never brought her up before," Tay Tay said, making them laugh.

"While we're talking about Sa'vere, you heard anything?" Becky asked.

"No, I don't even know if he's alive or dead," Tay Tay said as a tear ran down her face. Her cell phone ringing got her attention, and she quickly pulled it out of her pocket. Every time her phone rang, she hoped it was Sa'vere calling to say he was okay and coming home. She normally didn't answer unlisted numbers, but she wasn't taking any chances on missing Sa'vere.

"Hello? Yes, this is Taylor Brown," Tay Tay said into the phone. Marisol and Becky looked at their girl, anxiously waiting to see what was going on. Tay Tay looked like she was just listening to the caller. Then a still look covered her face.

"Nooooo, not my heart!" Tay Tay said, dropping the phone on the desk. Marisol and Becky could hear the doctor still talking on the phone, and they heard his words as clear as day.

"Ma'am, I'm so sorry for your loss . . ."

Discussion Questions for *Along Came A Savage*

1) What did you first think about Savere?

2) When did you first realize something was up with Mesha?

3) What did you think of Tay Tay hosting a BBQ and introducing Savere to her family?

4) Do you think Savere told TayTay about Mesha at a good time?

5) Were you surprised that Trell wasn't loyal?

6) What did you think about Savere and TayTay's threesome with Nicole? Was it messy or a power move?

7) Who did you think was behind the shooting of Tay Tay and Alisha at the liquor store?

8) Which do you think hurt TayTay more, the betrayal of her friend or the loss of her fortune?

9) What do you think about Tay Tay hooking up with Marisol and her mother, Juanita?

10) Tay Tay yells out, "Not my heart" in response to the phone call she gets. Who do you think the caller is referring to?

11) All of the characters seem to have a lot of determination when it comes to their plans and schemes. Who has the most and why?

12) Who's the most cutthroat?

13) Who's your favorite character?

14) Which character do you dislike the most?

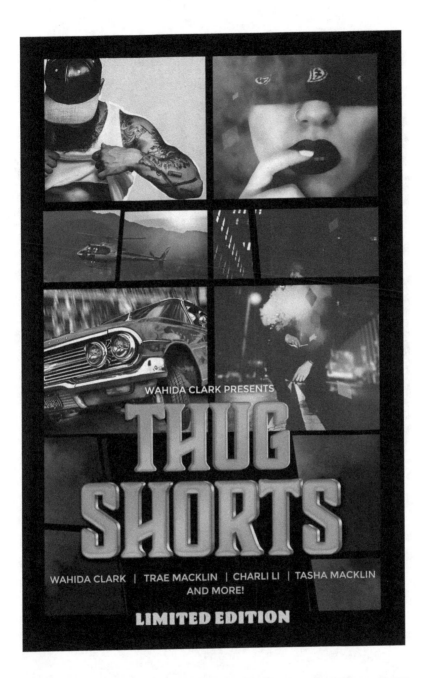

IN STORES NOW

WWW.WCLARKPUBLISHING.COM

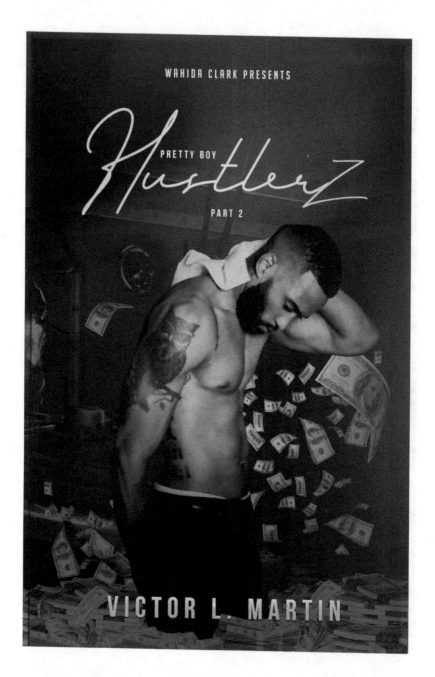

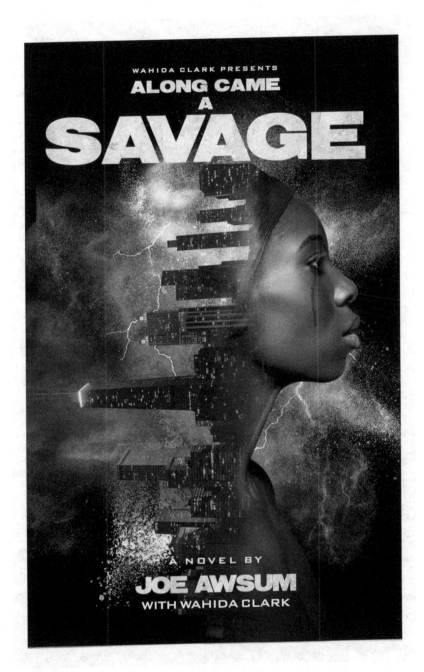

WAHIDA CLARK PRESENTS

SINCERELY THE BOSS

A MAFIA THRILLER BY

WAHIDA CLARK & AMY MORFORD

IN STORES NOW

WWW.WCLARKPUBLISHING.COM

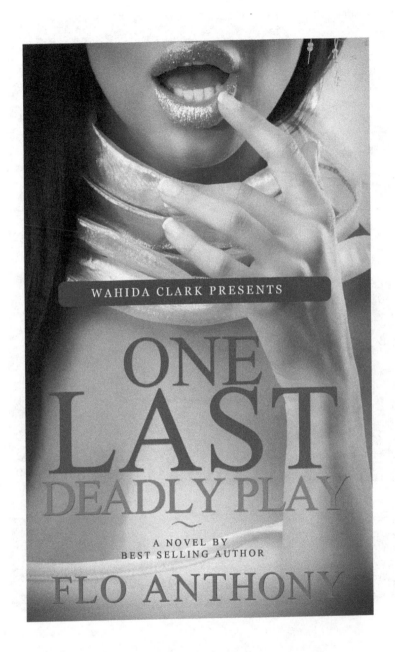

WAHIDA CLARK PRESENTS

ONE LAST DEADLY PLAY

A NOVEL BY
BEST SELLING AUTHOR

FLO ANTHONY

IN STORES NOW